THE CHRISTMAS EGG

THE CHRISTMAS EGG

A SEASONAL MYSTERY

MARY KELLY

With an Introduction
by Martin Edwards

Poisoned Pen
PRESS

Introduction © 2020 by Martin Edwards
Copyright © 1958 by Mary Kelly
Cover and internal design © 2020 by Sourcebooks
Cover illustration © by Mary Evans Picture Library

Published by Poisoned Pen Press, an imprint of Sourcebooks,
in association with the British Library
P.O. Box 4410, Naperville, Illinois 60567-4410
(630) 961-3900
sourcebooks.com

Originally published as *The Christmas Egg* in 1958 in
England by Secker and Warburg, London.

Library of Congress Cataloging-in-Publication Data is on file with the publisher.

Printed and bound in the United States of America.
SB 10 9 8 7 6 5 4 3 2 1

CONTENTS

INTRODUCTION

The Christmas Egg, first published in 1958, is an unconventional Christmas crime novel by an unconventional writer. Mary Kelly was one of the most talented British novelists to write crime fiction in the post-war era, coming to the fore just before P.D. James and Ruth Rendell appeared on the scene. Having risen rapidly to the heights, she abandoned the genre after publishing a mere ten books over a span of eighteen years. Her disappearance from the scene was as mysterious as it was complete; she did not publish a novel after 1974, even though she lived until 2017.

This was her third book. Like its predecessors, *A Cold Coming* and *Dead Man's Riddle*, it featured Detective Chief Inspector Brett Nightingale. In the run-up to Christmas, he is confronted by the puzzle of the death of the elderly Princess Olga Karukhina, who had fled her native Russia in the wake of the Revolution. But this is not an elaborate whodunit in the tradition of Agatha Christie or Dorothy L. Sayers. Nor is it a police procedural novel of the kind that John Creasey had popularised in the 1950s. Kelly's principal focus is on the study of character and on the idiosyncrasies of British society.

The idea for the story came to her after she was sent, in error, a set of books about Russia to review. The books were meant to be sent to Marie-Noelle Kelly, and this prompted Mary Kelly to read the work of her not-quite-namesake. This in turn led her to attend an auction of Fabergé eggs. Her knowledge of Islington, an important setting in the story, came from evening walks in the neighbourhood after she and her husband had visited the opera at Sadlers Wells.

When, eight years after its original appearance, the novel was finally published in the U.S., the eminent American critic Anthony Boucher lauded it in his column in the *New York Times*. Noting that Nightingale was an amateur tenor, he described him as an "unusually attractive" character. For Boucher, the book was "fascinating as a stage in the development of an important writer, and a pleasing entertainment in its own right." *Kirkus Reviews* also approved the novel, pointing out that the story involved "more pursuit than procedure," and saying it was "easy to read, fast to follow, with no remission of interest."

Mary Kelly's love of music is evident in much of her fiction, including *The Christmas Egg*. She was an enthusiastic singer, a mezzo-soprano with an extensive knowledge of lieder, capable of singing Schubert's song cycle from memory. Brett Nightingale's wife, Christina, was an opera singer, and Mary gained insights into the life and work of professional singers from Monica Sinclair, a member of the Covent Garden Opera Company who was Sir Thomas Beecham's preferred choice as contralto. Critics who shared Kelly's devotion to opera, and derived particular pleasure from her work, included two notable commentators usually associated with the classic whodunit rather than the psychological crime novel, namely Boucher and the composer Bruce Montgomery, better known as the detective novelist and *Sunday Times* reviewer Edmund Crispin.

The Christmas Egg consolidated Kelly's developing reputation as a quirky, intelligent crime novelist, but she was never interested in following fashion or working to a template. Later, in an excess of modesty that seems typical of her, she would describe the three Nightingale books as "sins of my youth." She wrote a novel without Nightingale, *Take Her up Tenderly*, which was rejected and never published. Her next book, which appeared in 1961, was very different, and it heralded a breakthrough in her literary career.

The Spoilt Kill was set in the Staffordshire Potteries, and had a workplace setting as memorable as it was unusual. The protagonist was an enquiry agent called Hedley Nicholson, but he was as unlike, say, Sam Spade or Philip Marlowe as Nightingale was unlike Freeman Wills Crofts' Inspector French or Ngaio Marsh's Inspector Roderick Alleyn. The book was critically acclaimed and won the Crime Writers' Association Gold Dagger for the best crime novel of the year, which was presented to her by Sir Compton Mackenzie. Given that in winning the prize, Kelly's book edged out John Le Carre's *Call for the Dead*, which introduced the now legendary George Smiley, the scale of her achievement is clear. She was promptly elected to membership of the prestigious Detection Club at the age of thirty-four; later, she became the club's secretary.

In reviewing *The Christmas Egg*, Boucher expressed the hope that Nightingale would return. What he (like almost everyone else) failed to realise is that, in a very oblique passage in *The Spoilt Kill*, Kelly had effectively killed off her first series detective in a car crash. Nicholson reappeared in her next novel, but he, too, was quickly abandoned. After that, she concentrated on writing stand-alone novels, and although her style was too understated for her ever to achieve bestseller status, she retained a devoted coterie of admirers. Edmund Crispin was among them, enthusing over *Write on Both Sides of the Paper* (1969): "her insights into human behaviour are tethered, wonderfully effectively, to the availability of spending money and the frequency of buses... Such conscientiousness may sound dull. In fact, however, it is all in a flight with the gentle, witty, profound acuity with which her characters are treated."

Yet there was something willful, as well as something admirable, about the way that, throughout her career as a novelist, Mary Kelly defied the conventions and commercial imperatives that guide the fortunes of almost all writers. Her publishers, not surprisingly, began to despair of her. So did some critics. Even her admirers admitted to some frustration.

An example was H.R.F. Keating, who opened an essay about her books in *Twentieth Century Crime and Mystery Writers* as follows: "One of the best contemporary British crime writers, but: such must be the verdict on Mary Kelly." Keating regretted the fact that she published so infrequently, and felt that she skimped sometimes on plotting, but emphasised that "there is enormous pleasure to be got from her books...what propels the reader through the pages is...the sheer excellence of the writing...from her very first sentence Mary Kelly observes so meticulously, describes so exactly and economically. Hers is a never-blinking eye."

Mary Theresa Coolican was born in London on 28 December 1927. She was educated at a convent and at Edinburgh University, where she met her future husband,

Denis Kelly (to whom I am indebted for sharing his loving and fascinating memories of her). After marriage and graduation, she worked as an auxiliary nurse and, like Denis, as a teacher; her first permanent post was as a teacher of Latin and English at the Convent of the Handmaids of the Sacred Heart of Jesus in Beckenham.

She enjoyed detective fiction, including the novels of Michael Innes and Dorothy L. Sayers, and the clear structure of the classic genre appealed to her; she often likened the Golden Age of Murder between the wars to the era of sonnets and sonneteers. At one point, her publisher promoted her as "the new Dorothy L. Sayers," but this was wide of the mark. Mary Kelly's writing was nothing like Sayers's, far less Christie's. Satisfaction with the plots of her books always eluded her.

For a novelist with such gifts and potential, *That Girl in the Alley* (1974) marked a low-key and anti-climactic end to her career as a published novelist; thereafter just one short story appeared, in an anthology in 1976. She decided to set her next book in Prague and researched the manufacturing of cellos for the background. Unfortunately, she felt dissatisfied with the new novel, and although she kept working at it, off and on, over several years, she never finished it.

Mary Kelly enjoyed socialising with fellow crime writers; her friends included such disparate characters as Patricia Highsmith, Anthony Berkeley, William Haggard, Josephine Bell, John Trench, Joan Aiken, and Michael Gilbert. At one point, when Michael Innes had lost interest in the Detection Club, she persuaded him to re-engage. But she became deaf relatively early in life, and as time passed, she lost touch with her colleagues and the genre.

Instead, she pursued other interests. She and Denis were

keen botanists, and she enjoyed decorating and gardening. They started renovating houses, selling up, and starting all over again, before eventually settling in Bath. In her seventies, she decided to write another book. The inspiration was the nursery rhyme "Ding Dong Bell." The story was to concern a drowning in a well in Surrey, and was meant to be slyly comic. Regrettably, she did not finish it before illness intervened.

As a writer, Mary Kelly was one of a kind. It's clear from reading her work, including *The Christmas Egg*, that she admired courage and honesty, and these are qualities that she manifested in her personal life. There are no locked room mysteries in her novels, no elaborate puzzles or plot twists, and no eccentric crime-solving genius. But in their quiet, polished way, her best books deserve to be ranked as crime classics.

—Martin Edwards
www.martinedwardsbooks.com

Part One

DECEMBER THE TWENTY-SECOND

Princess Olga Karukhin was lying on her back in her bed, a narrow iron contraption with a hard mattress. The khaki greatcoat and blankets which served for covers were scarcely raised by her bony old body. Her grey head rested on a greyer pillow, across which a sluggish winter fly crawled by stops and starts, attracted by the greasiness of the shawl wrapped round her shoulders. Princess Karukhina once had been used to lying in a carved bed inlaid with mother-of-pearl, between silk sheets changed daily, covered with down quilts and white furs. The walls of her lofty bedroom, sprayed constantly with rose-water, had been set with Wedgwood jasper plaques. Whole pelts of Polar bears had lain like ice floes on the glassy floor. The dark cramped room where she now lay was both sleeping and living room. The walls were shoulder-rubbed, the single rug curled at the corners, there was a pervasive smell of biscuits gone soft. The door of a wardrobe hung askew above the wedge of newspaper that had held it shut; in its mirror a tilted reflection of window and sky was dimming to a London dusk.

In the midst of this squalor the Princess lay still, absolutely still. Even when the inquisitive fly crept into her ear she did not stir. She did not feel it, for she was dead.

———

"I think," said Detective Chief Inspector Brett Nightingale, "we'll stop here in the High Street. There wouldn't be room to turn in Bright's Row. Back to that van."

The police car reversed gently and came to a standstill. Nightingale stepped from the back into the northern end of Islington High Street. He had seen it before only in daylight; by night it appeared even more of a survival from the past. Its narrow curving course and pavements sloping to a central runnel recalled the village long engulfed by the city. The high, flatfaced buildings crowded on either side, their ground floors of tiny shops bedizened at this time with dusty Christmas decorations, belonged unmistakably to London; but to the last century. Nightingale looked at the tawny window, full of umbrellas, by which he stood. 'Cane Repairer' was embossed in white letters across the glass. About two hundred yards away the Green, the village green, what remained of it, was flanked by a Music Hall. He remembered an undertaker's, with coffins and brass urns illuminated in the window; and in suggestive proximity a shop sheathed with blue and white enamel, advertising that a long-dead proprietor had been 'Agent for Female Pills, by the King's Letters Patent, 1743.' Nightingale shrugged, and shivered. His breath curled away from his nose in a vapour. If the cold weather tightened its grip, he reflected, they could have skating on the Thames as well.

He put his hands in his overcoat pockets and walked away from the car and the cane repairer's shop, turning off the patchily lit High Street into the cul-de-sac of Bright's Row. The left side of the road was a fenced bombed space; the right side, a short terrace of small, crouched houses, reminiscent of pictures in social histories of the nineteenth century. Nightingale looked along the empty street, at the luminous red and green and flowered squares of thinly curtained windows. At least the neighbours seemed to be minding their own business. Possibly, at the advent of the police, some of them were even removing evidence of it. The quiet was almost blatantly discreet.

Number thirteen was the last house but one. Lights shone behind drab curtains on both floors. The front door was open, and Nightingale stepped from the pavement over its threshold, bending his head to avoid the lintel. Nodding to the detective who rose from his seat on the bottom stair, he paused. From behind a slightly open door on his left issued the reasonable twang of Sergeant Beddoes' voice. It flashed through Nightingale's mind that Beddoes must have made an exceptionally sarcastic and immovable school prefect. He tapped on the door in a rhythm that was a sign between them; and after a couple of seconds, Beddoes came out.

"Didn't ask you in," he began quickly in a low voice, closing the door, "because she's rather upset just now. Mrs. Minelli, downstairs tenant. She made the call."

"Don't apologise," said Nightingale. "When did you arrive?"

"Half past seven."

"Where's the division—"

"Three youths breaking into tobacconist's, assault behind the Green Man, and a bad crash in the City Road, so he said would you please excuse him for the moment as I was here already and he's terribly undermanned, and he'd love to see you any time at the office."

Nightingale smiled. "All right. Shall we go up?"

The stairs were covered with cracked linoleum, and creaked as they climbed. Nightingale trod warily.

"Do you know," he said, without looking round, "I left as soon as I had the call, and I came straight here. Eighty-three per cent of the lights were against us, I worked it out."

"Busy just now for slipping them," observed Beddoes. "Good lecture?"

"Well—sordid but intriguing. He'd just finished when they rang. I'm glad you were available to come in advance—if their guess proves right—"

Nightingale paused for a moment. He had said, without thinking what he was saying, that he was pleased. It was true, but he hadn't meant to give voice to the feeling; since the real reason for it was that working with anyone less coolly irreverent than Beddoes made him feel that he was going to break out in a rash.

"Who's in this room?" he asked. "The photographer?"

"And Cobb and Telfer."

Nightingale pushed open the door and went in.

"Lord!" he exclaimed, stopping.

"East, West, home's best," said Beddoes. "Well, you can see—"

"I can't see a thing by this soupy light. Undrape the lamp."

Making a resigned face, Beddoes unpinned a piece of brown cloth which had been shading the glass bowl of gaslight.

"That's better," said Nightingale, "functionally. Aesthetically, a good deal worse."

As he spoke he moved across to the bed and looked down at it. "Has the doctor been here?" he asked.

"The division's."

"How long dead?"

"Seven or eight hours, perhaps. No violence. Bed wasn't disturbed."

"He didn't alter the face? No, I see. Went out quite peacefully, then. Still, the thing seems rather a stretched coincidence."

"Coincidence with what?"

Nightingale raised his eyes to meet those of Beddoes, clear, pale blue, ambiguously innocent and knowledgable, with innocence predominant at the moment in the form of an inquiring stare.

"I've been told," said Nightingale, trying not to smile, "that the Division diagnosed theft, Hampstead class. That's all. You've spoken to them—perhaps you'd let me have a few crumbs of information."

"Well, first," said Beddoes meekly, "it was just the Divi's sixth sense. Walked in the room, so I heard, stopped in his tracks, sniffed—figuratively—and spoke the oracular word. There was only the wardrobe door hanging open, as it is now, otherwise all serene—apart from the body. He had a scout round, and found *that*." Beddoes pointed to a large wooden trunk which stood in the middle of the floor. "It was under the bed, the position's chalked. You'll see the dust is brushed off the top in two patches. Divi immediately said 'Drooping blankets—lifted it to avoid marking the floor, and rubbed the top clean.'"

Nightingale bent to examine the trunk more closely. "Very fine, isn't it?" he remarked. "Decidedly out of keeping with the room. All right to open?"

"Yes, but it's empty, was when the Divi unlocked it."

"Good Lord! Locked it after them, does he think?"

Nightingale went to the table at the head of the bed. A sheet of paper, clinically white in the surrounding murk, had caught his eye when he first came in. On the paper lay a key and a length of dirty string.

"Divi found it round her neck," explained Beddoes. "Mrs. Minelli says she was never without it. The loop was large enough to be slipped off."

"But it's been untied recently," observed Nightingale, "and only that once, I think. The kinks and clean patches of the old knot are quite distinct. Still, go on."

"While underlings soothed Mrs. M. with tea, Divi nipped down and asked the people next door if they'd seen anyone or anything odd hanging around today. The old granddad at the end, he's always at home, he saw a green van outside about ten-thirty this morning. Took it for a gas van, swears he saw a North Thames Gas Board poster stuck on the side—but they could pinch that from a showroom. He didn't notice anyone enter or leave, inattentive old bat. According to Mrs. M. there was no call for gas men to come here. She didn't ask them, and if they'd been expected upstairs she'd have heard about it."

"Laundry at Hampstead and TV repairs at Golders Green. Always something where bags and bundles wouldn't look out of place. Perhaps the men were coming to mend *that.*" Nightingale pointed to the gas fire in the hearth. Three of its six jets were stuffed with corks.

"Domestic economy," said Beddoes.

"But at Hampstead and Golders Green there was obviously collusion with servants who flitted. Who let them in here? Or could they just walk in? But who told—"

"Wait a bit. You know her name?"

"Carrikin. Rather odd."

Beddoes frowned and shook his head in an aggrieved way. "Karukhin," he pronounced, elegantly.

"It's only what I was told," retorted Nightingale, nettled. "Since you went on that Russian course you've been unbearable. Why don't you transfer to Special Branch?"

"Run round seeing some nob doesn't bruise his backside? Boil me first!"

"All right, all right. Karukhin. A real Russian? I mean, by birth?"

"Yes. Came over after the Rev according to Mrs. Minelli. By the way, she's all right, Mrs. M. Even the Divi gives her the clear. Ex-waitress, naturalised '39, in the nick. Had to work in a hospital in the war, and stayed there. Deserted by husband in '41. Simple, devout, and all the rest. I've been talking to her."

"So I gather."

"Go in her room, and the first thing to hit you in the eye is the ikon over the mantelpiece. Reproduction of the Virgin of Vladimir." Beddoes turned a transparent gaze on Nightingale for a moment. "She calls it a holy picture. Apparently one day in an air raid Mrs. Karukhin came on Mrs. M. saying the rosary on her knees in the passage. No words passed, and Mrs. M. thought no more of it till Mrs. K. appeared holding the ikon, handed it over and pointed imperiously at the mantelpiece. Up it went, pronto, and up it stayed. Mrs. M's convinced it diverted the bomb to the other side of the road. This ikon, by the way, has a chased gold frame stuck with emeralds and rubies the size of marrowfats," Beddoes explained with attempted nonchalance.

"Oh?" Nightingale surpassed him. "Sure?"

"If it's brass and glass then the Divi's wrong too. He saw

it first. That's when he decided to let you know. Remember they took all that horrible shiny china from Hampstead."

"Nymphenburg porcelain, yes. So there seems to be a line in objets d'art as well as jewels—assuming that there was anything more up here, and that these are the same people. Certainly it's unusual to keep a trunk entirely empty, especially if there's not much cupboard space in your one room."

Beddoes brought something out of his pocket, unwrapping a piece of paper. "One day after Mrs. M. had taken some shopping upstairs, Mrs. K. gave her a brooch, similarly deeming explanation superfluous. Mrs. M. thought it flashy, so she never put it on except before taking other baskets up, so's not to let Mrs. K. think she disparaged her present."

He dropped the object he had unwrapped into Nightingale's outstretched hand. It was a very dark amethyst, about an inch square, elaborately cut, within a border of small diamonds; the whole being mounted on a gold frame and pin.

"Not a bad little nut, is it?" said Beddoes.

"You must have winning ways, that she let you take it."

"But she doesn't know the value! When she said it was flashy, she meant Woolworth's."

"And doesn't know the ikon frame is gold?" Nightingale was sceptical.

"Well, you know what it is. These people see gold plate on the altar from the year dot. They get acclimatised. They know, and they don't know."

Nightingale looked from the brooch to the figure in the dingy bed.

"Slightly unbalanced," said Beddoes, following his glance. "Never set foot outside the house in case the Reds got her."

"Hence Mrs. Minelli's shopping? I assumed she was

bedridden anyway, or at least too feeble to get out. Is this fear of the Kremlin of recent growth, or was there a predecessor to Mrs. Minelli?"

Beddoes paused. "Ivan. Her grandson. He who sleeps behind that screen and wedges his wardrobe door with the *Greyhound Express.*"

"Beddoes! You casually mention this *now*, at this stage, after minutes of piffling—well, not quite. But go on, since you've managed to get it out."

"He's a clerk at St. Pancras station," said Beddoes, in injured tones, "been there twenty-five years."

"How old, then?"

"Around forty. Well, you can see his grandmother must have been getting on for ninety. Anyway, there's nothing against him at work, the Divi checked that quickly. May root something out when they have time to do it more thoroughly, but on a superficial estimate he's slow and slightly stupid but honest. On duty today from nine to five-thirty as usual, and he had lunch in the canteen with one of the bods. No one who was sounded mentioned abnormal behaviour today, which they probably would have done if there'd been any to notice. Doesn't seem to have any cronies. However, he drinks. Mrs. M. told us that, not the station people. In spite of her modesty I gather she often had to provide for both of them when Ivan had swigged his wages at a couple of sessions. He was afraid of grandma—so was Mrs. M. incidentally—but not enough afraid to stop him having terrific rows. Mrs. M. could hear, but not understand. They carried on in Russian. That was another reason why Mrs. M. didn't flaunt the brooch. She felt Ivan would have been a bit cheesed at gran doling out largesse while he gasped for a pint."

"What about the ikon? If it's such an eye-catcher—"

"He never went in her room—strictest propriety. And you can't see it from the door."

"Oh well. Ivan hasn't shown up yet? Or will he be at the pub?"

"Not finished yet," said Beddoes, with relish. "Mrs. M. came home from work and shopping about six-thirty. Some ten minutes later she heard someone come in and go upstairs. She knew it must be Ivan because no one else has a key to the front door, apart from herself and the landlady—old girl of sixty-eight, living at Epping for twenty years, so can we wash her out? Anyway, Mrs. M. heard Ivan call—the point being that Gran was so scared of Reds that she bolted herself in the room all day, except for trips to the communal cold water tap in the kitch downstairs and the communal lean-to lav, and wouldn't unbolt till you'd knocked and declared yourself. Mrs. M. was lighting her fire. She heard Ivan moving about overhead, and thought of taking up the shopping. She hadn't gone up with it as soon as she'd come in for two reasons. First, there'd been no light in the upper window. Nothing to alarm her in that. It was often like it, only meant Gran was asleep. Second, she wanted to wait for Ivan because he'd have the money to pay her—she hoped. Just as she thought this she heard Ivan charge downstairs and out. She supposed he'd gone out to get something he'd forgotten. In about five minutes she went out to her kitchen and noticed that the Karukhin's door was open and the light was on. That was odd, because of Ivan being out and Gran's Bolshevik neurosis. Mrs. M. slipped up to see if she was all right—and there you are. She ran out and dialled 999. Call came in at six fifty-two, patrol arrived six fifty-five, and the divi followed at seven. Called us at seven-twenty. Mrs. M. was in a terrible state at first, because she'd asked for the police. Said she never thought that Ivan had probably run out to do the same thing, or else to fetch a doctor. When he didn't come back she was more upset than ever—frightened at the implications, maybe."

"Anything between her and Ivan?"

"You haven't seen Mrs. M. I know tastes vary—"

"Taste counts for nothing. You have to forget your own standards in the exercise of our charming duties. It couldn't have taken Ivan an hour to come home from St. Pancras, so I suppose he dropped in for a quick one on the way. All right, then. What have you done, besides chat with Mrs. Minelli?"

"First, sent out A.S. for Ivan—fortyish, about five foot eight, thin, fair, grey eyes, reddish face, blue chalk stripe suit, a cough, inclined to asthma, bad teeth—"

"And you expect him to cavil at Mrs. Minelli? Never mind. All stations? That's rather drastic as yet. No, I suppose not, if he's on the run. But it did sound as though he were taken by surprise."

"Why *hasn't* he called us, or a doctor, in that case?"

"True."

"And I've said not to take him in but just to tag him, in case he leads—"

"Good, good. Anything else?"

"Telfer looked at the front door lock. Nothing. No wax, no scratches."

"Anyone can get a copy of their own key cut, and pass it on. Even Mrs. Minelli. Well?"

"I thought you'd probably want *that* taken for analysis."

Beddoes pointed to a table set by the wall. On an ancient green cover stood part of a wrapped loaf; the top edge of its rind was sticky where it had obviously been cut with the same knife as had delved into the tin of syrup and had scraped the last of the margarine from the crumpled paper which also lay there, together with a saucer of sugar cubes and two cups stained with dribbles of cocoa.

"Looking for dregs of a sleepy nature in the cups, I take it," said Nightingale, "or in one cup, at least. What meal would this be?"

"Ivan's breakfast, Mrs. M. says. Gran never took anything but the cocoa."

"Come on, Beddoes, what's the big surprise? I can see you swelling with it."

"Just a trifle I happened on," said Beddoes, becomingly. "Don't raise your hopes. Look. On the table beside the bed, a book of devotions. On the fly leaf, here, you see, there's some writing in pencil, done a good while ago, I should imagine."

"Russian?"

"Yes. This top lot's a hymn, as far as I can make out. Religious verses, anyway. Quite in order. But the line at the bottom—know what it says?"

"No, Beddoes, I don't, but I should like to draw on the fund of talent at my disposal—"

"It says 'A. K. Majendie, twenty-eight Fitch Street, London.'"

Nightingale was silent. The words dropped like stones into the tank of his memory, disturbing the reflections of his past, which rose, jostled and sank, undisciplined by chronology. A girl with a yellow coat and a yellow switch of hair, sitting on a bombed space beside a shop during a sunny lunch hour; a velvet trayful of glitter in a shop window, and a woman looking at it, her back turned to him, her black hair twisted in a coil, Christina, his wife, before she was his wife; the girl, with the yellow hair braided round her head, seen from across the street, leaning into that same window to remove some delicate object.

"Majendie's," he said aloud. "Let me look at that line. Thanks. Why write an English address in Russian script?"

"Habit, perhaps."

"I thought she might want to keep it from anyone not knowing Russian. It seems at a glance to correspond with the hymn, but we'll get them to find out whether the two lots were written at about the same time. The pencil's pressed off on the inside cover from the hymn, the single line isn't. But that may be due to a variation in the paper, or something."

"Ivan could speak Russian."

"But had she taught him to read it? If he came to England with her, after the Revolution, he'll have been here since he was a small boy, even a baby. And if she was a recluse, she won't have exerted herself to launch him in the Russian colony. I don't see any books. Where would he have learnt to read it?"

"He did come with her," said Beddoes, "according to Mrs. Minelli—not that she knew from experience, but so he told her, and there's no reason to doubt that. Also, Mrs. M. says this was their first and only home. Certainly this was Ivan's address when he started at St. Pancras. No relations, to Mrs. M.'s knowledge. No friends, for that matter."

"I see," said Nightingale. "Would you go and ask Mrs. Minelli whether she ever posted letters for Mrs. Karukhin." Nightingale took considerable pains with his pronunciation of the name. "If so, to whom, if she can remember."

Beddoes went off in silence. Nightingale put the book on the table, removed his gloves, and leaned his arms on the mantelpiece, withdrawing them hastily as they encountered a scurf of matches, shoelaces, sugar cubes, coppers and other small dusty objects. He examined the shelf warily. Under the dust he could see innumerable sticky rings and some recent ones less thickly coated. Beside an alarm clock stood a half-used tin of condensed milk and a packet of cocoa, ingredients of the morning drink, which plainly was always made in the cups as they stood on the mantelpiece, handy to the kettle resting on the double gas ring at the side of the hearth. He supposed that the ring represented the Karukhins' sole cooking facilities, unless they chose to trudge up and down stairs with dishes from Mrs. Minelli's kitchen. And that dilapidated wash-stand, with its chipped enamel basin and jug, was where they washed. A cake of soap lying on the marble slab was dry and flaky, suggesting infrequent use. As he looked round the room he saw confirmation of his guess about the cooking, in that Cobb was carefully turning out of a corner cupboard an assortment of foodstuffs, mostly in paper bags. It was an advantage of his present rank, Nightingale reflected, that the investigation of crumby, mousy cupboards and dingy beds by him, personally, was a matter not of necessity but of choice. By being selfish enough to seize that advantage he was denied the satisfaction of discovering some factual clue. He had merely to supervise the people who might find the hair, the pin, the print, which could make or break. But he was the one who, later, was supposed to make sense of the collected facts. He wondered why he had ever wanted the responsibility of drawing conclusions that could so easily be wrong.

Beddoes returned, looking rather dejected. "As far as Mrs. M. knows," he said, "she never sent out a single letter and never received one."

"It doesn't matter. What I'm going to do now is to ring Runciman. You never met him, did you?"

Beddoes shook his head. "Left before I came. Strong on Slavonic Studies?"

"That's right. He was at King's with me. I want to ask

him if the name Karukhin ever appeared in the course of his studies or duty."

"I've asked Records, as far as the duty part's concerned. And if they weren't naturalised they'll have had to report in the war, so the divi's checking that. There may not be anyone still there who remembers or knows them, and it'll take some time to unearth records."

"Why not go straight to the Home Office? Ask whether these Karukhins are aliens or naturalised. They can look up both registers simultaneously, and whoever gets the right file wins. I'll see to it. Now, in case some form of Press life puts in an appearance, you'll have to let them know the old woman's dead, unfortunately. Give them to understand it's just an ordinary sudden death, and if they want to know why, in that case, we have a hand in it, let them think it's the death that's being queried, without any gloss of robbery. Do you think Mrs. Minelli's told the neighbours much of the home life of the Karukhins? Or about the ikon and brooch?"

"I'll ask her."

"Do. And ask her if she hasn't some friends or relations she could stay with for a while. If she hasn't, tell her to say absolutely nothing to anyone but you or me, and to lock that ikon out of sight. Exert your charm, Beddoes. She might even let you take charge of the ikon till everything's blown over, which would be perfect."

"If it's the Hampstead people, they'll be watching the papers for even a tiny para. What will be their reaction to the news that Mrs. K's dead? They haven't caused anything like that before. Think they might get a shock and clear out double quick?"

"It probably won't be news to them."

"But if they came in the gas van at about ten-thirty, and she's only been dead seven or eight hours—"

"She was in a death sleep when they came, perhaps. And Ivan may have run out to tell them. Anyway, we can't keep it out of the papers if they do get hold of it, and I don't think it will make any difference to the Hampstead people. Success is going to their heads, I dare say. You know—'Exceeding peace had made Ben Adhem bold.' Carry on as you are doing. You can have the car that brought me here for sending things back to H.Q.—the cups, the book, anything that you may find. The car's in the High Street. I'll send it along. Oh, and the mort van will be coming, of course. When you've finished with the room for the time being, close it off. Then make a beginning with the neighbours. Anything at all about the Karukhins. There's no pressing need for me to see Mrs. Minelli, since you have. It would be a mere formality."

"Thank you!" Beddoes answered irony with a well-gauged bow.

"For myself, I shall ring Runciman. And then," Nightingale concluded, kicking aside a sprouting potato which, dislodged by Cobb's poking, had rolled across the floor, "I'm going to see Majendie."

He went out into the street with no more than a glance of curiosity at Mrs. Minelli's door. Later, he would visit her, chiefly to see the ikon; the gold-framed, gem-studded ikon, which thieves would never have omitted to collect had they known of its existence. He was sure, now, that there had been thieves; the same thieves as at Hampstead, or at least under the same direction. He was dealing with their third manifestation. They were a new set; but they planned well. After the second, Golders Green, episode, of which he'd been notified within two hours, he'd organised raids on the premises of every known large-scale receiver, with a speed and strength that had enormously elated his pride; until each party had reported a dismal blank. The very importance of the thefts made their disposal through small dealers almost impossible. Therefore a new hand was at work; presumably, a whole new ring. What really astounded him was that none of the others had split. Since he knew that neither fear nor chivalry would deter them from slitting an upstart's throat, directly or by means of a hint in the right place, he was forced to conclude that they were as much in the dark as he was. He kicked a cigarette end angrily into the gutter. A blight seemed to have fallen on the faculties of the informed and the informing. He frowned. One very good source, having been treated to a savage beating and left more dead than alive on a waste lot near the Bricklayer's Arms, was now immured in St. Thomas's hospital; a fact which no doubt had its relevance. But he hadn't much hope of doing anything without information. He entered the High Street, sent the police car into Bright's Row, and walked through the nearest gap into Upper Street. He felt as if he had emerged from a tunnel into daylight. The broad road was bright with neon, electricity and sodium, full of noise and movement from busy pavements and a double stream of traffic. The old High Street, bypassed by the century, atrophied in gloom; yet it ran like an undertone beneath the throbbing prosperity of its supplanter; a sort of *memento mori*.

He went into a telephone box, planted as if expressly for his convenience, and looked up Runciman's number. As he dialled he wondered nervously whether the complaint which had caused Runciman's premature retirement might not have carried him off; nearly a year had passed since he had last had occasion to speak to him. With relief he heard Runciman's own voice, and pressed the button.

"Hullo," he said, "it's Nightingale. Yes, I know. I'm sorry. I've been so busy. How are you? Good. And your wife? Thank you, very well. Listen, I want your invaluable help. Does the name Karukhin mean anything to you? What? *What?* But wouldn't there be more than one family? You're sure? All right, I'm sorry. But I'd no idea. Look, I didn't think there'd be as much as this. I can't wait now, I'm on my way to see someone. Could you 'phone it through to the office? All you can. Tell them I want it copied accurately this time. They'll understand the reference! Thanks a lot. Seven four—oh, you remember. Don't forget to charge *them*. I'll ring you again later. Thanks. Goodbye."

He dropped the 'phone, lifted it again, and dialled the number of his own home.

"Hullo?" he heard Christina say. He was about to reproach her for not answering with the number, when a belated awareness of the tone of her voice stopped him. "Hullo, Chris," he said. "I'm afraid I've had a call. It's all local so far, but God knows when I shall be in. So don't wait up. I'm sorry."

"Oh." There was a pause. "All right."

"Is anything wrong?" he asked.

"I've broken my cameo," she said, unsteadily.

"Oh, darling—" Brett stopped. He didn't know what he could say. The brooch was not valuable, but it was pretty, and she had been attached to it because she couldn't remember a time when she had been without it, and because it had belonged to her mother. "How did that happen?" he asked awkwardly.

"It was lying on the edge of the piano. I'd taken it off—I don't know why—and I just put it down without noticing where. Then I went to close the top of the piano and the prop slipped, somehow, and fell in, and the lid dropped—"

The inconclusive silence suggested tearfulness. Brett felt it would be heartless to comment on the injudicious placing of the cameo. "I'm sorry," he said. It was all he could think of saying. If he had been at home he could have comforted her in silence, or at any rate with words which simply could not be said coldly into a telephone. The silence was continuing. "Chris?" he said.

"Yes?"

"Oh—I wondered if you were still there. I must go. I *am* sorry," he repeated, desperately.

"Yes, all right." Her voice was flat. "Goodbye."

"Goodbye."

Brett lowered the receiver. At this moment he almost envied those glib rattles who could reel off their tongues long spools of pretty consolations for feminine disasters. What their minds were doing, of course, apart from congratulating their own good humour in patronising the weaker sex, was anyone's guess. But though silly witless women might be flattered, Christina would be neither deceived nor gratified at such attention; at least, he hoped she wouldn't.

He pushed out of the steamy box into the street. The bitter cold could not neutralise the café-emanations of fish and chips and vinegar, in which the road seemed steeped; but it served to enhance the seasonable contents of the shops—tangerines, nuts, fir trees, boxes of frilly crackers, row on row of trussed turkeys lit by a ghastly glare of fluorescence. *Nature, in awe to Him, Had doffed her gaudy trim.* Human nature was more than making up for climate deficiencies, and preparing to commemorate the event with its customary wallowing. Brett looked along a chain of windows, gaudy with red and silver, dabs of cotton wool, strings of fairy lights. His mind dwelt on the sombre browns of the Karukhins' room. What, if any, incredible fairy lights had sparkled in that trunk? He began to imagine a Christmas tree in a platinum tub, its emerald branches festooned with diamonds; gold ikons piled at its foot were the presents.

Presents. He still had nothing for Christina, and with only two shopping days left he was beginning to feel frantic; especially as each thing he thought of seemed on reflection trite, trivial, or dully utilitarian. But the sight of a bus, stationary at the stop, put the matter out of his head. He ran to join himself to the end of the queue.

———

"You know him well by sight?" he said into his office 'phone, sometime later. "You're sure? He's at the Haymarket. He's bound to be in a decent seat and it's a good exit to watch anyway. You might catch the last interval, but don't bother if not. See him home—he'll be in a taxi—and the minute he's indoors let me know. Mind what you're doing, now. I've just come from his house and I think it's watched—or I am. Either way it's bad. If you don't see him at all, let me know that too, as soon as you're sure. Yes, I'll be here. Thank you."

He rang off. On the whole, he felt it was he who had been the object of someone's curiosity. He'd not been aware that he was followed until he'd rung the bell at Majendie's own door; but then the sensation had come on him very strongly. A glance up and down the street had shown him several people on both sides, all walking purposefully and appearing in no way suspicious. That apparent innocence meant less than nothing to him. He knew by instinct that one or even some of the passersby had marked the visitor awaiting admission. What helped him to conclude that he was, or had been, of greater significance to them than the house was that when he'd left, a few minutes later, there was no one near enough for observation. They might have hidden, but he doubted it. He'd walked into Marylebone Road, taken a taxi, and had ordered it first, as an evasive precaution, to Baker Street, then back to the Place, which had been remarkably empty. So he had returned to the office, not in the least flattered to have roused such interest.

Majendie, according to his housekeeper, was at the theatre. Beddoes, according to the Division, was following Ivan round the pubs of Islington. Nightingale poured himself a cup of tea, and settled thankfully enough to read sheets of Runciman's transcribed notes.

———

KARUKHINS—obscure origin. Family liked to say there were Karukhins at Kiev, but first definite appearance in medieval Vladimir. Survived Tartar attacks by servility to conquerors, Muscovite dominance by cunning and astuteness. Great leaps of boldness and rapacity during Chaos preceding accession of Michael Romanov. From Peter to Catherine, followed policy of ingratiation with autocrat, resulting in immense political influence. During and after Napoleonic wars, emphasis subtly shifted to acquisition of money alone instead of power first and money as corollary. By end of nineteenth century, Karukhins owned, thanks to strategic marriage campaigns, estates in Ukraine, Crimea, Vyatka, producing immense quantities of grain, fruit and timber respectively. Also smaller estates outside Ryazan and Yaroslavl. (1861 Emancipation of serfs. Karukhins less affected than many, because biggest and most productive estates were in the south, where less land received by serfs, whom landlords found it cheaper to payoff.) Also owned emerald mine in Urals. Residences, apart from those on the estates:—villas in Caucasus, Crimea and Monte Carlo; flat in Paris; house in Moscow; palace in Petersburg.

1893 Prince Sevastyan Karukhin married Countess Vyestnitskaya. Prince S.——handsome, stupid and dissolute. Interest in politics stopped short after automatic endorsement of furthest extremes of Reaction. Ruled by two passions—first, gambling, hence much time at European casinos, Monte Carlo being the favourite. But for second passion, gipsies, might have lived always abroad. However, no gipsies so pleasing to him as those of native land, therefore a great frequenter of Tzigane restaurants, esp. Villa Rodé, and Yar when in Moscow.

Princess Olga, however, ruled palace and all in it, including Prince while he was indoors. Inflexible will to dominate. No unseemly commands or disputes, but compulsive pressure of a look from narrow black eyes. Model of strictest fidelity to husband. Too proud for intimates, but lavishly hospitable to many. Servants well rewarded and cared for, and her voice never raised. Yet all feared Olga Vassilievna.

Son and only child, Ilarion, domineered from infancy by mother, grew up vapid and nervous. Degenerate Karukhin strain swamped all traces of Vyestnitsky maternity, except for querulous obstinacy, shadow of Princess Olga's will. Eruptions of this obstinacy ignored by the princess, even when directed against herself, since never occasioned by any but most trivial matters. She also turned a blind eye to son's sexual dissipations—precocity inherited, like empty head and handsome face, from his father. Apart from these instances of calculated freedom, mother ruled him in everything.

1913 Prince Sevastyan died of a stroke (induced, some said, by rumour that Tsar had granted a liberal constitution) and Prince Ilarion became nominal head of the house. In reality, as everyone knew, it was Princess Olga.

1914 Prince Ilarion twenty. Nothing changed for him by the war. Being of noble birth, had no obligation to serve, or alter habits of extravagant indolence. Social life of capital continued, if somewhat altered by absence of those who felt morally compelled to try to alleviate Russia's misfortunes.

1916 Autumn, Prince Ilarion married girl of mother's choice, Irina Shcherbinina, youngest daughter of a general, delicate docile blonde.

1917 Outbreak of March Revolution and abdication of Tsar were events which not even a Karukhin could disregard. Prince Ilarion shocked and horrified, but no idea of leaving Petersburg, where engaged with dancer of Imperial Ballet. Went round saying 'revolt' would soon be quashed and autocracy restored. Concluded that, since he'd taken not the smallest part in conduct of the war, provisional Govt. could have no quarrel with him (apparently never thought that as they were intent on a more vigorous prosecution of the war effort, he might have to *do* something). Princess Olga less sanguine but indomitable, so Karukhins stayed precariously on through worsening situation till Bolsheviks seized power in November.

Princess Olga foresaw irrevocable end of Tsarism and imminent catastrophe for them and their kind. Prince Ilarion, on the other hand, refused to accept this, and was moreover too infatuated with his dancer to think of leaving. He and his mother in major conflict for first and last time. He disregarded her dire warnings. Furious at his blind obduracy, she left him and contrived her own escape to the Finnish border, travelling by road in weather and conditions that would have daunted a less determined mind. She took son's wife with her, but

Princess Irina had neither will nor constitution of her mother-in-law, and was also seven months pregnant. Within a week of reaching Finland she died in giving birth prematurely to a son, who survived and was christened Ivan.

From Finland Princess Olga arrived in Sweden in the summer of 1918, with the child. For the next two years she lived there in close retirement, apparently making no attempt to communicate with her son or with anyone she had known in Russia. During that time was published news of the shooting of the Imperial Family at Ekaterinburg; and, as a mere incident in the savage course of the Civil War, of the shooting at Petersburg, in reprisal for some White atrocity, of three hundred class enemies, among them Prince Ilarion Karukhin.

———

Nightingale pushed the papers aside and sipped his fast-cooling tea. The only person in that story whose plight moved him was Princess Irina, the delicate docile blonde. He smiled at the detail, and the brief covering message from Runciman.

"The general stuff I knew," he read, "but the tittle-tattle is father's. I've put it all in on the chance of its being usable. You can rely on its accuracy. The old man's eighty, but his memory's as clear as a bell. His authority for the Swedish episode was a friend who was at Stockholm at the time. She worked up quite an acquaintance with the Brit. Col. there, then seems to have faded out. Let me know what happened to the Karukhin remnant if you find out—and if it's O.K. for private release, the old man would be interested!"

Nightingale nodded. Runciman's father had held some position at the Petersburg embassy for several years before the Revolution. His mother had been Greek. So it was hardly surprising that Runciman himself had found the study of Eastern Europe congenial. Nightingale had forgotten what was his special field. He could remember that Runciman had once laid himself open to mockery of almost a year's duration because, asked by a superintendent for help in a newspaper quiz, he had been at a loss for the date of the battle of Agincourt, and had excused himself with the plea that it was outside his period. Nightingale made a note to have the usefulness of Runciman's derided specialisation brought to that superintendent's knowledge; only as he was now considerably more than a superintendent it would better be done by devious means.

He rang the divisional office. "About the Karukhins," he said. "It seems likely that they've lived at Bright's Row since the early twenties. As he would have been only three or four years old when they came, he must have attended a local school. Find out which, please, and if there's anyone on the staff old enough to remember him. Of course, the schools will have closed for the holiday, but your people probably know the caretakers, and they can get the headmasters' addresses from them. There's always the education office as a last resort. See what you can do, anyway. Also, he drinks, I believe. Does he patronise a particular pub, do you know? What about that one behind Sadlers Wells, the Empress of Russia? No, perhaps not—a sort of *lèse majesté*. Well, a chat with the landlord, if you can find him. I gather his present stopping place isn't a regular haunt or you'd have looked sooner. And I'd like more from St. Pancras than an alibi and a negative character. Anything at all about him. All right. As quickly as you can."

The 'phone started to ring as soon as it was settled. Majendie, he thought, picking it up. It was Majendie; rather, he was the subject of the call; he had just returned from the theatre. Nightingale glanced at his watch. It was late, but not too late. He would see him now.

———

There was a pause in the argument of three men at the bar, followed by a sudden but unrelated hush in general conversation. The impassive, heavy-chinned barmaid pulled the handles for a mild and bitter. Prompted laughter barked distantly from a radio to which no one was listening.

Beddoes glanced with assumed idleness at Ivan Karukhin; and seeing that he was handing over the counter money for yet another drink, returned to his ostensible struggle with the evening paper's crossword, a puzzle of such puerility as not to deserve the name. He gnawed the end of his pencil, an exercise fostering an illusion of mental labour and dispelling the taste of beer, which was a liquor he could not teach himself to like, although considerations of anonymity and expense had caused him to order and swallow half of pale ale.

He stared round the walls of the public bar as if searching for inspiration. Those walls were composed, to waist level, of reddish wood. The upper part was adorned on one side by glazed tiles which formed pictures of pseudo-classical half-draped women, and on the other two, including the bar, by plate glass with an engraved border. The fourth side consisted of the frosted windows. The ceiling was almost completely hidden by an oppressive mesh of paper chains and bells which hung in a pall of smoke unruffled by the draught that seemed to Beddoes to be cutting through his ankles.

Nightingale, he thought, was probably swigging surreptitious sherries by a roaring fire in the plutocratic jeweller's house. In thirteen years, he calculated, he would be as old as Nightingale was now, and would have risen as high; in the meantime, he was a silly sergeant, who had only himself to blame for his present discomfort. As soon as Ivan was reported to be in the Derby Arms he had rushed down there himself; which would have been all right if it had stopped at his taking a look, to make himself familiar with the fellow. But the detective who had discovered Ivan and who had watched him thereafter, had mistaken Beddoes' single glance of recognition for a dismissal. He had, of course, his own lines to watch. Quite a separate matter, in fact, had taken him into the Derby. That he had spotted Ivan was incidental and a stroke of luck, especially as he must have heard the message by the narrowest margin, just as he was leaving the station to come on duty. For him, Ivan's description had been superfluous; he knew him, as did certain other local detectives, from having to spend almost as much time on duty in pubs as Ivan spent voluntarily. And the division, which had its Christmas rush together with and as a result of the one in the outside world, could not have been expected to transfer someone solely to the Derby for the sake of saving Sergeant Beddoes a walk in the cold. Thus Beddoes repeatedly tried to indoctrinate himself.

He let his eyes come to rest on Ivan, who was sitting against the plate glass wall, a little apart from the groups of talkative drinkers. He was obviously very drunk. Beddoes thought he must have been swilling steadily almost since he had run out of the house in Bright's Row. He was surprised that Ivan had found energy to come so far from home, some ten minutes' walk; for even considered as a product of his environment Ivan was a poor specimen. Although the cut of his cheap suit was skimped to a degree, it lay loose and awkward on his puny frame. The skin of his face glistened, stretched over inflamed, almost ulcerous flesh. His straw-coloured hair looked wet, though when from time to time he left his seat for the bar a greasy patch was visible on the plate glass where his head had rested. Beneath a straggling moustache his mouth permanently drooped, thereby increasing the slackness of his chin. He had a nasty spattering cough, which appeared not to trouble him. But nothing appeared to trouble him. He stared blankly at the ground, raising his glass and swallowing the beer in it with dull regularity.

The sight reminded Beddoes of his own glass. To his surprise he found that he had slowly emptied it, and to his dismay he saw that the clock stood at ten to ten. He couldn't in decency sit on the side for the next forty minutes or more without buying another drink. He stood up. Beer was out this time. He refused to go on being a martyr. He went to the bar and ordered rum. Faint strains of a carol concert piped from the indefatigable radio. The equally indefatigable bar proppers had abandoned politics for a more general discussion. One of the three was buying the round which had fallen due to him; a small man with a face like a battered nut, in which blue eyes glittered like chips of glass.

"Three the same, please, Daff," he said briskly, raising his cap more in gesture than in deed. "No, Jim, he don't know, he don't see it," he went on to his cronies, almost without a break. "But what odds tween Bill knockin' off a couple a pots a paint—which he did, I admit, which he did, Jim, you needn't spit about like that—an' the ol' man knockin' off in the afternoon to go to Twick'n'am? *Or*," he jerked the word in with great vehemence, on a rising note, "the ol' man takin' a couple a men off to do 'is car for 'im—*in* the firm's time. Eh Jim?"

Jim, who had evidently suffered a setting down in recent

disputes, merely looked mopy, and raised his glass to the speaker in a swooping gesture.

"No, Jim!" The third man was older than the others. His face was red, he had an enormous Stalin moustache and bushy grey eyebrows, under which his dark eyes twinkled as if in ceaseless anticipation of the point of a joke. "Alwiz the same. Alwiz 'as bin. Alwiz will be. One lot a rules for them an another for us. Same everywhere. Can't change it, 'aint no use tryin'. Once you swaller that, boy, life comes a lot easier."

Having delivered these maxims in a slow rich voice, with each pause given due length for the point to sink home, the third man tilted his glass and drank most of the contents in one draught.

"Sides," the nut faced man resumed, "what they think'll 'appen to their paint if they leave it lyin' about? Put temtation in people's path. Just like Daff," he added suddenly, grinning at the barmaid. "Eh Daff?"

The woman's face betrayed no flicker of emotion; she might not have heard the sally. Her long chin and inscrutable eyes and heavy bronze make-up made Beddoes think of some kind of Indian.

"'Ere, Joe," began Nut-face.

Beddoes didn't hear the rest. He had so much ado not to laugh at the moustache man's name that he turned away. So it happened that he saw Ivan rise from his seat and sway towards the bar. He came to rest between Beddoes and the group of three. Without a word he pushed the empty glass at the maid and groped for his pocket, supporting himself all the time on the counter with his left hand.

The barmaid stared stonily at him and made no move. "I don't think you'd better have any more, sir," she said in a flat way, making it a statement rather than a recommendation.

Ivan simply waited, as if he hadn't heard, gaping at the glass. Since he appeared quiescent, at least for the moment, the barmaid busied herself elsewhere. But Beddoes saw that her move was designed to establish relations with potential assistants. Having fetched something which she kept under the counter to a position by the three men, she leaned across and touched Joe's arm.

"You going to have one of my raffle tickets, Mr. Pearce?" she asked heavily.

"Raffle tickets, my dear?" Joe turned with an almost courtly inclination. "What for?"

"First prize, hamper and five pounds, second, turkey and bottle of whisky, third—"

"No, no, Daphne, I meant, what's the charitable object?"

"Same as usual—Dr. Barnardo's."

"Ah. Yes, I don't mind a couple, Daphne."

The maid lifted out the things she had brought from further along the counter; a book of tickets and a large silver and blue cardboard egg.

Nut-face laughed. "Bit early, Daff? Goin' a raffle the egg too?"

She was still forming her slow reply as Ivan lurched round, staring.

"I ain't got it," he squeaked.

It came as a shock to Beddoes, to hear a prosaic whine issue from Ivan, instead of elegantly broken English or fluent Russian as he'd irrationally expected.

There was a pause. The mantle of authority fell quite naturally on Joe.

"Ain't got what, old cock?" he rumbled, his fruity bass at once firm and soothing.

Ivan was silent. His eyes passed hazily from one face to the next. Beddoes met him with indifference. Ivan shook his head and turned back to the counter. He extended a shaking hand for his expected drink, the money for which lay where he had left it.

"Go on, Daff," Nut-face urged the hesitant barmaid. "One more can't do no 'arm." He grimaced and winked behind Ivan's back to indicate that he, personally, would insure that it should not.

"'Ere, mate," said Joe magisterially, nodding support to Daphne, "'ave one with us. One more on me, eh boys? An' we'll make that the lot. Same agen, please, Daphne. An' what's yours, chummy? Chirrup an twitter?"

For all his fuddled condition Ivan realised quickly that he was being offered a drink. He managed to collect his money and put it back in his pocket without dropping it, then edged along the counter to attach himself to the main party. Whether he intended to comply with Joe's cunningly inclusive admonition that this drink was to be the last, or had even understood it, Beddoes doubted. But the ruse had succeeded in so far as it had lured Ivan to a position from which the three guardians of the pub's peace could at least try to sweep him out the easier way, in a general comradely exit. And Ivan was suddenly very anxious to be comradely, either because to stand him a drink was to make him a friend, or, as it seemed to Beddoes, because he found something in the three men to reassure him. He seized his beer and gulped some down, as though aware that if he didn't reduce the level quickly the shaking of his hands might cause wastage. His face became animated, although the direction of his eyes remained unsure. He even attempted a feeble grin. He opened his mouth.

"I see it," he said.

Beddoes looked cautiously round the room. Its occupants

were engaged in talk, either in pairs or in groups. He and Ivan, perhaps rather unfortunately, were the only solitaries. No one appeared to have noticed what was going on at the bar. Indeed, Ivan's voice was so weak and wheezy that Beddoes imagined it must be inaudible beyond the range of his immediate circle.

"I see it," he repeated, breathlessly. "I told 'im what it look like. How could I tell 'im unless I see it?"

"No, that's right, mate," agreed Nut-face, with a pessimistic glance at his friends.

"I told 'im," continued Ivan, heedless of a need to clear his throat. "I told 'im all about it." His expression grew maudlin. "Ah, it was lovely," he sighed.

"What was, mate?" asked Nut-face patiently.

"The egg."

Nut-face tapped his forehead to the others. "What egg?"

"The Easter egg. I told 'im. All white an' glittering, lovely, like ice an' frost an' stars."

"Blimey!" Nut-face raised his eyebrows. "Bleedin' poet!"

"Sounds more like a perishin' Christmas egg." The morose Jim spoke up suddenly. "Yes, I reckon thass what that was—a perishin' Christmas egg, eh Joe? A Christmas egg."

It was only by the repetition that he showed satisfaction with his wit. His face was as lugubrious as ever.

Nut-face burst out laughing. "'Ere, Daff!" He leaned across the bar to communicate the *mot*, which was still being mumbled by its author.

"Lovely," said Ivan. He raised his eyes, and Beddoes saw that they were swimming with tears. "An' I lost it, I lost it. I lost all of it." The tears ran down his cheeks.

"Oh gorblimey!" muttered Nut-face in disgust. "What about it, Joe?"

"Cheer up, cock," said Joe, laying a paternal hand on Ivan's shoulder. "Why don't you go 'ome?"

Ivan made such a convulsive movement that Joe, evidently thinking he was about to be sick, stepped hastily out of range. Ivan was not sick; but in a moment his former vacancy returned. He swung his back to the man who had bought him his drink, which he had not yet finished.

Beddoes moved unobtrusively away. He went back to where he had been sitting, picked up his newspaper and pencil and left the pub. At any minute, he felt, Ivan also would be leaving, either voluntarily or propelled by Joe and Co. He walked a few yards along the main road, then stopped, and with great deliberation took out a cigarette and stuck it in his mouth. He covertly blew out three matches to prolong the business of lighting it, but the fourth he let alone. Then he dropped his paper, contriving in letting it fall to catch the edge of the centre page and fan it wide apart, and to place it so that he had to turn back to face the pub. He picked the paper up carefully, folding it into a tight roll; and, as he finished, was rewarded by the sight of the pub door swinging open and Ivan staggering out; alone.

He didn't come along the main road towards Beddoes, but turned into Tamplin Walk, the narrow alley at the corner of which the Derby Arms was built. The far end would join Goswell Road, thought Beddoes, sauntering after him. This was probably the quickest way to Bright's Row. But did Ivan want to go back to what he'd fled, the squalid room and the dead grandmother? Perhaps he'd forgotten. Perhaps his feet had of long necessity grown independent of his head, and carried him willy nilly in the right direction from any pub in the district. If he did go home, the division could look after him. And the best of luck, thought Beddoes, viewing with disfavour the alternative prospect of snailing round Islington till the small hours. He wouldn't risk losing sight of Ivan by phoning for someone to take over, and as he could recognise none of the divisional detectives except the man he'd relieved at the Derby he couldn't hope to meet help on the road.

Come on, Vanya, get a move on, he muttered under his breath, watching Ivan's unsteady progress down the ill lit lane. Vanya's hide, unlike his own, appeared to be seasoned by drink and impervious to cold. That rum had been a good idea. Two would have been even better. Nightingale, no doubt, was still toasting himself in the jeweller's armchair. Beddoes waited a moment; then, at enforced leisure, strolled through the set of iron posts which marked the end of Tamplin Walk and which Ivan had encountered with some confusion.

They had emerged into the brightness of Goswell Road, near the great junction with City Road. Ivan, with drunken recklessness, lunged off the pavement and struck out on a long diagonal across both lines of traffic. Beddoes rolled up his eyes, suppressing the hope that a heavy lorry would take Ivan off his hands, and followed; only he kept with propriety to the pedestrian crossing, which lay like a tape measure straight across the double width of the converging main roads, divided only by the island with its lavatories and huge yellow road signs. Oxford, S. Wales; Slough, The West, they promised. Beddoes, launching himself on the second half of the black and white strip, looked to his right, but not as traffic drill. Up and down the City Road, in and out the Eagle. Where was the Eagle? Not far down you could look from the road into the grey water of the Basin, banked by wharves, factories and dumps. Within the gentle throw of a stone a wooden boom slanted across the surface; a clump of rushes sprouted in the centre of it, and in that solitary patch of vegetation a pair of swans had built a nest. That was the nearest thing to the Eagle that he knew. But he wasn't going to see that tonight. Ivan was going straight on. It began to look as if he meant to go home; and, not before time, he was going faster. There were few people about. The street was quiet; but not dead, being dotted with bright windows, outward sign of the warrenlike nature of the old houses which rose flat and sheer from the pavement. Beddoes could and did look down into snug carpeted basements, with coal fires glowing in the grates. Coal from the cart didn't burn with that still brilliance, he knew; but the great railway depots of Somerstown were not far away. He averted his eyes from the tantalising prospect of so much untouchable comfort, and studied the erratic course of Ivan. The faster he wished to go, the wider he rolled. One of the houses, shaken by past bombing, was shored up by two large beams, their bases embedded in the pavement. Ivan skirted the first, swerved, and went under the second, as though he were starting a figure of eight in a country dance. He was trying to run. He passed, or rather, narrowly missed, a young couple coming towards him. Quite unconcerned, they minded their own business. Beddoes watched them approach. They walked with their arms round each other, the girl's head resting on the boy's shoulder; yet they were walking fast, and discussing something between themselves with a brisk, businesslike air. They were foreigners, Beddoes realised, as their incomprehensible speech bubbled into his ears. Perhaps that accounted for their uninhibited pose, taken for granted and adhered to regardless of mood. In this part of London many foreigners lived. Beddoes thought they could do a lot worse, Islington had some kick, some independence in it. He wouldn't mind living there himself. In Bright's Row, perhaps? He smiled. There were blacker spots than Bright's Row in some fancy-named outflung suburbs. And what was wrong with these roads, where the houses were well kept, well curtained, well fired, respectable without insipidity—

Now where? he asked himself sharply. Ivan had swung into a side street which would lead him away from Bright's; and as Beddoes turned the corner his heart sank. The road branched; and at the fork stood a small pub. If the meandering muzhik went in there, Beddoes decided, he would ask the landlord for use of the 'phone and would ring the Division. They could, they'd *have* to, send someone round while Ivan was swigging. He loafed along in Ivan's wake. A white and tabby cat ran across the road and disappeared into the darkness of a bombed patch. There was a contractor's board stuck inside its fence. Soon a sharp block of flats would rear abruptly over the old houses, which were smaller in this road, and darker. There was no one out but Ivan and himself; and Ivan was heading for the pub door.

Beddoes began a long systematic curse; then checked. Vacillating Vanya had thought better of it. He reeled down the road to the left of the pub, a road which marked a swing back towards Bright's. Beddoes tagged on resignedly. He supposed he ought to be thankful that Ivan was too drunk to suspect he was followed, that he never happened to look behind him. Unaccountably, Beddoes felt the desire to look back himself. He did, carefully. Two men, shambling towards the pub. Another cat, streaking low to the ground. Nothing. Ahead, Vanya was developing quite a turn of speed. He was nearly at the end of the road, where Beddoes perceived railings and trees. What was that? A park? Gardens?

Ivan reached the corner and turned left; and from the right

hurtled a soapbox on wheels, narrow tyreless rims clattering over the cracks of the pavement. Two bicycle lamps were fixed to the front. Power was provided by the energetic foot work of the small boy at the back, while his partner, the driver, was responsible for steering and simulating the noise of a piston engine in top gear. With a sound like the disgruntled meeeow of a wild cat, he waved his hand up and down to signify that they were to stop. The contraption came to a standstill within an inch of Beddoes' toes.

"Got the time, please, mister?" asked the driver, staring up at him.

"Time you were in bed," observed Beddoes civilly, looking at his watch. "Twenty past ten."

A gasp of horror met this information. "Thanks, mister. Come on, Tim," said the driver, all in one breath.

Beddoes watched them dashing off. "You ought to have red lights on the back," he called after them. "You're breaking the law!"

Tim stopped the furious working of his feet, turned, cocked a finger-gun and emitted two sounds like steam escaping from a train. At which, Beddoes supposed with a smile, he ought to topple slowly to the ground, clutching his stomach and grimacing.

He started, and ran to the corner. Ivan was gone. There was no sign of him, up or down the road. Without hesitation Beddoes crossed to the opposite pavement, flanked by the railings and trees he'd seen from a distance. He refused to give way to panic, though his heart was hammering; as yet there was occasion only to abuse himself as a triple cloth-head. Ivan couldn't have gone far in those few seconds. Perhaps he was in one of the houses, calling on a friend. The windows were all dark. The row seemed deserted. Beddoes peered through the railings into the spreading trees on his right. He jumped. It seemed to him for a second that he was standing on the brow of a steep hill, from the invisible foot of which rose many-storeyed tenements, layer upon layer of lighted windows. Then he understood. The hill brow was a sloping bank; what he took for a void of darkness was a strip of motionless water; and the tenements reaching from the depths were the reflected backs of tall houses perched on the treeless opposite bank. Now that he looked closely he could see, so still and mirror-like was the inky surface, that in what he'd thought were lower storeys the curtains and lamps were all hanging upside down. This must be part of the canal. Which canal? The Regent? The Grand Junction? Nightingale lived near a canal. Nightingale—what could he say to him? *I was watching some kids in a cart.* He walked on. The bank was so steep that the trees revolved in the corner of his sight as he passed them, willows with enormous sprawling limbs. A cat, the third, a black one shot suddenly through a gap in the eroded railings. Beddoes stopped. That wasn't the only movement. What was the matter with the lower storeys? The bright window squares were wavering, stretching and contracting. There was no wind. Something had dropped or fallen.

"Ivan!"

He shouted it. Russians, canals, suicide. He shouted to the empty street, forcing himself through the gap in the railings, shouted formlessly as he stumbled down the bank, slithering, catching at branches and bushes, fumbling for the whistle in his pocket. Not there, forgotten, black mark, he thought; Ivan, Vanya, blast you, this isn't the Fontanka. He tore off his raincoat and flung it behind him somewhere, dragged off his shoes, grabbed his torch—remembered for once—and swept the beam over the water. There was the centre of the spreading ripples, close to the edge. With a despairing bellow for help to the backs of the tall houses, he threw down the torch and plunged in. He yelled for sheer agony. He was being stabbed, riddled, cut up. It was impossible, it was freezing. He couldn't stand it, he was going to get out. He went under, blind and groping, meeting nothing but swirling darkness. Yet he could feel it wasn't too deep, six or seven feet. He groped and groped. His heart was going to split in a second. He had to breathe. He burst the surface, spluttering and blowing. Why hadn't someone come? He had to have lights. He shouted, very breathlessly, and went under once again. He swam and groped, swam and groped, till lights began to ping on and off on his head. Suddenly he hit something soft, recoiled, choked on a gulp of water, and clutched material between his fingers. There was movement, a struggle against his hand. The grip wasn't right, he hadn't had time, hardly ever practised. They were sinking. He heaved, kicked, clawed—chin, shoulder, and got it. Now surface, he had to surface, to break out of all the bells and fireworks, up, back, and up. But clothes were heavy, Streatham Baths in trunks another matter. An inch, only an inch—but he couldn't, not with Ivan. Let him go, he thought. No. It was coming. He was through. He gasped, and swallowed knives. His body was on the rack. His legs were strangely feeble. The bank, now, he thought, the dry scratchy bank, with Ivan dead or alive, and soaked enough without the help of the canal. Regent or Grand Union? Moika, Fontanka, or Ekaterinski? Something rubbed his shoulder. The bank.

He dragged himself out, landed Ivan, rolled him over and collapsed on top of him, shaking, puffing and snorting. Why had no one come? He tried to call out and uttered an exhausted croak. He couldn't let Ivan die, not after all that. He heaved himself up and tried to press down on Ivan's back with arms like jelly fish. Swimming was obviously not his best subject, especially in near ice. One, two, wait, he thought. Come on, Vanya. One, two—

A meteor cracked his head open, a magnesium star split the darkness. Nuclear warhead, he thought sickly, and knew no more.

———

Mr. Majendie reminded Nightingale of a small fat silver-haired hamster; or perhaps a round silver teapot, spouting puffs of steam, was nearer the mark, including as it did the loquacity, so gentle and fussy and quasi old-fashioned. Nightingale felt more than a touch of scepticism. He didn't imagine that a leading figure in the trade of fine jewellery, objects of art, and antiques, had reached or held his position by conducting business in loving kindness. Majendie the plump household pet, blinking over the top of rimless spectacles, babbling per- siflage, inclining the head in urbane courtesy, was all the time marking the flaw, the crack, the fake; or concealing jubilation at an unsuspected treasure. From behind those innocent lenses could shoot a glance of extreme shrewdness, such a one as Nightingale had witnessed in the midst of Majendie's professions of surprise and regret. The professions were gen- uine, he thought, within the limitations of Majendie's speech. How distressing—thus Majendie received news of Princess Karukhin's death; but accompanying was a flash of great relief, not to say satisfaction, as if Majendie said to himself, and from his heart: how fortunate.

"It would be interesting to know," Mr. Majendie said now, stretching his short legs to the fire, "how our estimable police force discovered that Princess Karukhin had been a client of ours." He paused for a moment to peep invitingly at Nightingale, who smiled politely. "Ah, I'm not permitted, I see. Such a pity."

Mr. Majendie's face grew serious. "But the Princess," he murmured. "Dear me, how sad! One feels, you know, that an era has closed. And what an era! We shall never see its like, my dear sir. Never."

"No," said Nightingale in a neutral tone. Eras must close quite commonly for Majendie. "When you said that the princess was a client of yours, did you mean a former client?"

Mr. Majendie blinked sweetly. "She was still honouring us with her patronage. We called on her, you know, as late as last week."

"Not at Bright's Row?"

"Where else?"

"I'm surprised you knew of its existence," said Nightingale.

Mr. Majendie smiled slyly at him. "I didn't, I confess, until the princess wrote to me."

"Wrote? Through the post?"

"The Post Office generously conveyed the letter—on credit, as it were. The princess had omitted the formality of a stamp."

"I see. When did this come?"

"Some ten days ago—it will be filed in my office." Mr. Majendie paused. "She wrote, as you may guess, to offer for sale jewellery and various valuable objects."

"She'd sold to you before?"

"She *disposed* of some pieces in the early twenties—she had recently made her way to this country. A fine diamond and ruby brooch, I remember, and an enamelled watch— formerly the property, I believe, of Princess Irina. That was the only occasion, apart from this last, on which she availed

herself of our professional services. But of course I remembered her from Petersburg."

"Oh? You were there? When?"

"19—let me see, 1911 and 1912, those were the years I
spent in Petersburg. My father was a man of great wisdom,
and great foresight. He was expert in porcelain, you know,
but jewels are my great love—always have been. He saw that
when I was a mere youngster, and encouraged it. Wonderful
man. Liberal. Nothing of the narrow specialist in him. Sent
me abroad to study and gain experience. France, Germany,
Russia—unforgettable."

"And at Petersburg you met—"

"Fabergé. A great master, and a very charming, kindly
man. There were, of course, others. Britzin, Khlebnikov,
Tillander—I had letters of introduction to all of them. But
Fabergé, sir, was outstanding. I studied chiefly with Wigstrom,
Henrik Wigstrom, you know, one of Fabergé's workmasters,
I consider him to have been the greatest."

"And the Princess?" Nightingale tried to steer the conversation a little nearer his goal.

"But of course! That was how I was brought to the notice
of the Karukhin family. I remember going to the palace with
Michael Kulp—a German, you know, one of Wigstrom's
assistants. Such a privilege to be allowed to accompany him.
My dear sir, if you could have seen the Karukhin palace! So
difficult for young people to imagine the sheer lavishness of
that vanished age!"

"You went to the palace—"

"Indeed yes. Prince Semeon Karukhin built it, in the
days of Catherine, you know, but each generation added
something—the private theatre, for example, the Roman
Bath, the hothouses. Vast building! Two ballrooms, two

banqueting rooms, a whole chain of *salons*—one in which only Grand Dukes were received, another for princes, another for lesser nobles, and so on—*salons* for music, for chess, for tea, for fruit and lemonade."

"And the Princess?" repeated Nightingale gently, repressing a boorish desire to ask where the Karukhins had received tradespeople.

"Had ordered half a dozen parasol handles. We were submitting designs for her approval. How well I remember. Impossible at first, you know, not to be overawed. The Princess was a formidable person. She treated me, however, to a signal mark of condescension—addressed me in French, then and thereafter. Never forgot."

"You saw her again?"

"Several times—and her husband, Prince Sevastyan. He used to come to Fabergé for presents as a regular thing. So many did. His son, too, Prince Ilarion. I remember him spending a couple of hours deciding between two enamelled powder boxes for his mother's name-day gift. He preferred trinkets—his youth, I suppose. His father invariably gave jewellery—for the anniversary of their wedding-day, I remember, a magnificent parure of emeralds and diamonds. We delivered it on the previous evening. They were giving a ball—hardly a night passed, you know, but there was some form of assembly at the palace. Magnificent—roses and candelabra everywhere—and what beautiful chandeliers!"

Mr. Majendie, who was stretched almost horizontally in his chair, sighed nostalgically.

"So the name Karukhin alone would entitle a letter to serious consideration," said Nightingale, "even if there hadn't been the diamond and ruby brooch in the twenties, and even if the address were somewhat startling."

Mr. Majendie bowed his head. "There could be no question of ignoring it. My dear sir, you know Bright's Row. You may conceive the painful contrast to me—"

"You went yourself? In person?"

"Princess Karukhin demanded no less," said Mr. Majendie, looking over the tops of his spectacles. "Of course, I took the precaution to ascertain that the Princess did live there—though she had allowed the title to lapse, naturally."

"Did you go quite alone?"

"Upon instruction, yes. In any case, I judged it better to make the call in every way inconspicuous. I took a cab to Upper Street and went the rest on foot."

"She let you in herself?"

"Certainly. You mustn't imagine that she was enfeebled or bedridden. She appeared in excellent health and vigour, considering her great age."

"But I understood that she wouldn't let anyone in unless they knocked in a special way, and called out their name and business."

"That may be so. I had no such instruction. But then, you see, I was to arrive exactly at three o'clock or not at all. She wrote that she wouldn't receive me at any other time."

"So she was expecting you. That would be as good security as a codified knock. She could watch you from the window. She seems to have suffered a morbid fear of discovery and persecution. I suppose if she was hoarding family jewels—"

"My dear sir, she was hoarding a treasure," said Mr. Majendie impressively. "But I should say she was haunted not by the possibility of losing that, but by the fear of being carried off to Russia. Her son, you know, was shot. Yet in my opinion she didn't fear death. She hated the new régime so bitterly that she was simply determined to deprive it of further prey in the shape of herself."

"I should think the régime had enough to do without bothering to hook back the ones that got away," observed Nightingale. "But as she was accustomed to being a person of the first importance it probably didn't occur to her that her whereabouts, her very existence, could quickly become a matter of indifference to Red and White alike. Obviously, she had to live in obscurity for her safety immediately after the Revolution, and by the time she came to England the habit of secrecy was hardening into an obsession. I believe she went almost straight to Bright's Row. That was a pretty unbalanced thing to do. With the sale of some more of her jewels she could have lived in moderate comfort. She could have changed her name for security."

Mr. Majendie sighed. "Yes, I knew at the time—not where she was living, but that the catastrophe had unsettled her mind. She imposed on us—or me, rather—such tremendous conditions of secrecy concerning the sale of the brooch. Protestations of professional integrity and confidence were not enough, I fear, to reassure her. As for changing her name—pride would forbid, I think."

"In any case, once you accept the fact of an unsound mind, nothing need be logical. She went to you, plainly, in both instances, because your stay in Petersburg entitled you to her trust. Did you, in fact—" Nightingale reframed his question. "Were you able, this time, to help her dispose of her jewels?"

Mr. Majendie shot him a look as quick as any hamster's. "No, sir. That is, the matter was in suspense. The Princess, you see, asked for payment in cash, which was, naturally, not available on the spot. Besides, before committing the firm to such a considerable undertaking I had to consult my partners, one of whom was in New York at the time. I did explain that we were more than interested, and I promised definite acceptance of at least part within a few days. This satisfied her—knowing the firm, as you said, obviously carried great weight. I offered to have the trunk, in which, believe it or not, my dear sir, the objects were stored, transferred to our strong-room or a bank, pending negotiation, but she argued—very convincingly, one must admit—that as she'd kept it safe for forty years she could do so a little longer. There was nothing to do but leave. Of course, she forbade us to communicate with her in any way until we heard from her again."

"And you never did?"

"Oh, indeed yes! A letter arrived the very next morning—"

"Stamped?"

"No," said Mr. Majendie, with submissive deprecation. "It was not, however, to arrange a further appointment. The Princess had changed her mind as to the manner of payment. Instead of giving her cash, we were, if we decided to take part or all of what she offered, to make over the value by cheque, direct, to any school for the daughters of the nobility."

"What!"

"But that, my dear sir, was a cause widely supported by Russian ladies of wealth and family," said Mr. Majendie in surprise. "The Empress Marie Fedorovna—"

"Yes, yes," said Nightingale, recollecting himself. "I meant, it showed how much she was living in the past, in the Imperial Russian past. You would have been hard put to find a school that conformed to such an exclusive pattern in England now. Did you know that Ivan Karukhin, her grandson, lived with her?"

Mr. Majendie made a regretful little grimace, pursing his lips and putting his head to one side. "A young man whom, I feel, life has not treated kindly," he said. "The Princess remained, essentially, formidable."

"And do you know whether she was naturalised?"

"I'm afraid I've no idea. I wonder—" A gleam of cupidity appeared in Majendie's eye. "Ivan Karukhin, whom I have not met, is at present, no doubt, too distressed to appreciate his new position. But I wonder—"

"Whether he'll sell?" Nightingale paused. Basing his judgment on Majendie's behaviour and a knowledge of his commercial and social status, he had decided that Majendie was either right in the thick of the Hampstead people or completely innocent; no half measures. If he was involved, to tell him of the robbery would occasion him no more than secret amusement at the expense of the police; it would be no indiscreet revelation. If, as Nightingale considered rather more likely, Majendie was innocent, then he was of the sort reliable in co-operation. Discretion, being habitual with him, would scarcely need to be appealed to.

"I'm afraid," said Nightingale, "that the Princess's treasures are no longer at Bright's Row."

Majendie's eyes widened immediately. He certainly looked surprised; yet Nightingale would have sworn that his first fleeting reaction was again, inexplicably, one of relief.

"Not there?" he said, puzzled. "But he can't have sold already! She hadn't the remotest intention—regrettable as it all seemed—of letting him touch it. Ah—" He smiled wryly. "Unless, indeed, we have both overestimated the influence of Petersburg!"

"You're thinking that she'd approached other firms than yours, and had silently accepted a better offer? But we have reason to believe that she was robbed."

There followed what was for Majendie quite a long silence.

"Shocking," he said at last, "profoundly shocking. But, tell me, was her death—natural?"

"We don't know," said Nightingale. He paused. "But could you tell me, in detail, what she had? It would help us, to know what's been taken, and if we should recover—"

"Quite so, quite so. I made a few rough notes while I was at Bright's Row, though I could remember the more outstanding items. I drew up a full list for my partners, but unfortunately I haven't it by me. It's at the office. You wanted to see it tonight?"

Nightingale hesitated. There was a risk. He decided to take it. "No, thank you," he said, "tomorrow morning will be soon enough. When may I call?"

"My dear sir, at any time."

"Thank you. Could you also give a rough valuation?"

Mr. Majendie darted one of his sharp glances at Nightingale. "Why do you ask for that?"

"Because," explained Nightingale, incredulous that Majendie should need telling, "if there's a reward offered, someone may inform. *We* can't offer the reward, obviously, but we could co-operate with a firm of—"

"Of course, of course. But surely Ivan Karukhin would be prepared to indemnify—" Mr. Majendie stopped to look inquiringly at Nightingale, who said nothing. Mr. Majendie's face grew thoughtful. "Well, well, no matter," he said. "You shall have a valuation."

"An estimate from memory would be enough." Nightingale paused. "You spoke of a treasure," he reminded Majendie quietly, "and of a considerable undertaking."

Mr. Majendie frowned, and put the tips of his fingers together. "Yes—but it's very difficult—a treasure, certainly, especially to a lover of all forms of jewellery. But much of it, you see, would not have found a ready buyer—it belonged to an awkward period, not yet restored to grace by the turn of taste and fashion. Most of the pieces would have had to be broken up for the sake of the gems, and even then, a great number of those were rose diamonds, for which there's almost no demand in modern jewellery. Again, some of the pieces were silver set—and silver, you know, has quite lost to platinum and palladium. So when I spoke of a considerable undertaking, and the need to consult my partners, you must realise that it was in the sense of responsibility." Mr. Majendie leaned forward to poke the fire.

"Oh. You had no misgivings, afterwards, of the Princess's ability to keep her property safe? Perhaps if you had set a security officer to watch—"

"But my dear sir," objected Mr. Majendie in great surprise, "the trunk and its contents had not yet become *our* property. The firm, I am happy to say, was in no way dependent on the sale. Why should we have troubled?"

"I see," said Nightingale. He rose. "Thank you very much for your help. I'm sorry I had to call so late in the evening."

"Not at all, not at all. How pleasant, if duty were always so agreeable. Now if, tomorrow, I should be called out—I don't anticipate, but at Christmas one must be prepared for anything—I'll leave the list with my secretary, tell her to hand it to you personally."

"Your secretary—not the girl who sits on the waste site in fine weather?"

"No, no, dear me, no! That's Miss Cole, our youngest member of staff—came to us just over a year ago, straight from school. Charming girl, charming. So agile—hockey, you know, lacrosse. Only the other day someone knocked a Chaffers off a shelf—underneath were some pieces of faience brought in from Sotheby's, a most interesting pair of Strasbourg pigeon tureens. If you had seen Miss Cole move! Lightning, sir, positively lightning! Wonderful save. You frequent Fitch Street?"

Nightingale, who was wondering what a Chaffers might be, collected himself. "I've bought records from the shop next to yours," he said.

Mr. Majendie's face could not, probably would not, have altered more profoundly if Nightingale had uttered an abrupt obscenity. Nightingale decided to pursue the subject a little.

"I drove along Fitch Street this evening," he said. "I see from a notice they've put up that they're to extend their premises to that site." It occurred to him that Majendie's apparent dislike of the gramophone shop might be prompted by resentment at their having acquired a coveted space. "What used to stand there?"

"You don't remember Elliman, the florist? No. Poor fellow, never recovered from the blow—the bomb, you know. Lost all heart. Wouldn't rebuild, wouldn't claim war damage compensation—but wouldn't part with the lease. Amazing obstinacy. Died a couple of years ago, and the executors sold, of course. Uneconomic premises for a single business. Small, no egress at the back. We and the gramophone people block the way. What strange anomalies of building and planning exist in great cities. Fascinating. Rather dull, don't you agree, if everything were regular and symmetrical? London may be a muddle, but it has a heart, a lively beating heart."

"It certainly has," said Nightingale, thinking of the turbulent central divisions of the Metropolitan Area.

"You know," said Mr. Majendie, "had the Princess's trunk passed into my possession, I could have offered something of considerable interest to our phonographic neighbours. The Princess had two old records—oh, very old. Brought them away with her. She showed them to me. They were her favourites, she said, but as she's no means of playing them I might as well take them with the rest. Wonderful, and rather touching, that she should have preserved them for so long."

"Was she interested in music?"

"Devoted, my dear sir, devoted. She was a Vyestnitsky, and they were all musical. Her brother, Count Sergei—what an elegant man, by the way! I shall never forget his canes so long as I live. I was about to say, he had a collection of records quite famous at the time—which was, of course, the comparative infancy of recording. He was an enthusiast. So was Prince Sevastyan Karukhin. But not a pure enthusiast." Mr. Majendie glanced up at Nightingale as if assessing his fitness to hear an inglorious revelation. "He had, you see, to outdo his brother-in-law. That was *his* motive for collecting. He built a studio in which to house and play his records—nothing if not thorough. Converted the hothouses."

"How did he manage to do without those?"

"But the railways, you see, development of the railways," explained Mr. Majendie, unaware of sarcasm. "Fruit and flowers could be rushed by special train from the southern estates—often were, especially for balls and banquets. Kept them fresh on blocks of ice, you know."

"What were the Princess's records, can you remember?"

"I'm not much up with all that sort of thing. Let me see. Olimpia Boronat—does that convey anything to you? Or have I confused—"

"That sounds possible. She was a Russian soprano. What was she singing—The Last Rose of Summer?"

"That I can't remember. Now who was the other singer? A handwritten label—a man's name, French, I think. Something, I recall, that put me in mind of cigarettes—"

"Not—de Reszke?"

"Why, splendid, Mr. Nightingale! Well done, indeed. That's it. Jean de Reszke."

"Jean!" Nightingale's voice shot up several tones.

"But is he famous? I confess I've never heard of the fellow."

Nightingale looked incredulously at Mr. Majendie. He could believe that a young person might not know of Jean de Reszke unless they had certain interests; but he had thought that before 1914, which was the period of Majendie's otherwise receptive youth, names like Tamagno, Maurel and de Reszke were still bandied in society with as much facility as W.G. Grace and Kaiser Bill. That was the impression some people liked to give.

"Offered to the right party," he said, "a record made by Jean de Reszke would probably realise as much as one of the Princess's jewels."

"Astounding! Was he so wonderful?"

"I don't know," said Nightingale meekly. "He died when I was seven or so. He had a tremendous reputation. But the value of the record would lie in its rarity. I didn't know he'd made any at all. Perhaps it was done privately. By the way, he wasn't French, but Polish."

"Ah, you are interested in music. I have no ear for it. But tell me—did the thieves possess greater discrimination, or perhaps greater acumen? They took these records?"

"If they were still in the room when they called, yes. We haven't found them. But that doesn't mean that they knew the value of them, and I should be surprised if they did."

"I wish, Mr. Nightingale, I hadn't told you. You're disappointed, I see, to think how narrowly you've missed being able to hear that rarity."

Nightingale smiled. Denial was pointless. To the accompaniment of a great effusion of courtesies from Majendie he made his way out.

After Majendie's blazing fire and soft carpets, the street seemed colder than before. Nightingale shivered. Majendie was an old fox as well as a hamster. All that blinking bonhomie; that exaggeratedly fragmented, dated, affectedly preserved manner of speaking; all of it a fence to baffle the casual observer from a glimpse of his cunning, even ruthless, pursuit of business. It was like a false limb, in the use of which he had from long practice grown so proficient that it was literally second nature.

It didn't matter to him, Nightingale thought, unless Majendie was using the fence to hide something rather more than rapacity; and that he was still inclined to doubt. Would Majendie, if he were involved with the robbery, have admitted so much? Possibly; on realising that the police had found a link between himself and Bright's Row, he might have decided to play safe, admit to having been there, as was inevitable, and hope that the unknown clue would not compromise his explanation. Could that explanation be corroborated? No; except by Majendie's partners, who would be at best tainted witnesses. If the partners were innocent, was there any reason to suppose that a list of the Princess's belongings existed? Would Majendie now set to work to concoct one? And in the morning he would have to produce two letters from Princess Olga. That business of the stamps, or lack of them, suggested a fudged story; it was one of those touches by which someone in haste seeks to improve a fiction, but oversteps the bounds of discretion. Had he thought to obviate the post mark difficulty, forgetting that no stamp did not imply no post mark, that in fact there would be an extra Post Office printing to enforce the double charge? In any case, how many offices filed envelopes?

In spite of all this, however, Nightingale tentatively absolved him. He would be wary with Majendie, that was all. If the letters he handed over *were* forged, they would in time be proved so: and in that time it was unlikely that Majendie, secure in his lucrative business, would try to slink out of the country.

Meanwhile, he wondered, what was Beddoes doing about Ivan Karukhin? He made for a telephone box, glad enough at the prospect of its shelter. If there was to be any prolonged watching of premises in this affair, he thought, whoever did it had better be got up as a night-watchman, complete with hut and brazier; otherwise they might tender their resignation.

He dialled, and caught sight of his face reflected in the mirror. Why did all mirrors in telephone kiosks throw back such a ghastly glare? In them every complexion was livid, every blemish magnified. He heard the office answer, pressed the button and made himself known. Before he could say more, a spate of words poured into his ear—Beddoes, the canal, slugged, St. Thomas's. Without waiting to hear further he dropped the 'phone and drew a couple of deep breaths. He pushed open the stiff door, then hesitated. He hadn't thought to ask how badly Beddoes was hurt. But it didn't make any difference. St Thomas's, quickly, that was the main thing. He flung out of the kiosk and began to run up the road. Fool, ass, idiot! he silently apostrophised Beddoes, and urgently hailed a cruising taxi.

———

Beddoes had taken quite a nasty knock, although no serious damage had been inflicted. He was looking very white, and very unfamiliar in the bleached and roughly ironed hospital pyjamas; but he couldn't be prevented from reciting his adventure in a rather shaken voice. Nightingale had given up trying to stem the flood of disgusted self-derision. For Beddoes seemed to feel more mortified than physically uncomfortable.

"Then the last straw," he was muttering now, "wake up and find a damn great retriever yowling and sniffing all round you, as if you were some fat partridge—do they get partridges?"

"He sounds a very intelligent dog," said Nightingale.

"Yes." Beddoes closed his eyes. "Put it on the kids' telly. Saved a copper from bronchial pneu. Pity he wasn't going walkies a bit sooner—see what they did with Ivan the Terrible. Or pity he wasn't a bloodhound. Rub his nose on the bank and follow the trail. What are we doing—about Ivan?"

"Don't bother," said Nightingale.

Beddoes opened his eyes. "I'm all right."

"You don't look it." Nightingale felt that a little dashing of Beddoes' spirits could do no harm.

"You've never seen me without a tie, that's all it is," said Beddoes. "Young and vulnerable."

"All right, then. Apart from keeping our eyes open for him we'll drag the canal in case they just tipped him back."

"Shan't half be mad if they did. All my work."

"They mightn't risk using it again after you'd indicated its potentialities to us. I expect they realised you would come round, only they couldn't wait to help you to your feet. I doubt if they meant to put you out for good. And even then, your dead body on the bank would have drawn unwelcome attention to the canal in the end."

"Surprising, really, they didn't tip both of us in together. Simple solution."

"Not if they had nothing to hand to weigh you down," said Nightingale more calmly than he felt. "That's what's puzzling about Ivan. They threw him in, having presumably knocked him out first, yet left him to rise in time. It looks as though they acted almost on the spur of the moment, and certainly they must have been double quick about it. Yet I can't believe they met him by accident and just seized the chance to even up some score against him. And if they were looking for him, how did they know which way he'd be coming? If they'd been following him, they'd have seen you, and wouldn't have taken the risk. And if he turns out not to be in the canal, we'll have to assume they took him off in a car. They couldn't get far otherwise with a wet inert body. Then why not bring the car alongside him in the first place? Much easier and safer to hook him in."

"Thought it was suicide at first." Beddoes sounded weary. "Can't have been, I suppose, in the light of the rest. Tell you how to find out if he's in it—analyse a cup of canal water. If it's five per cent proof, start dragging. Christmas eggs!"

Nightingale stood up. "I'm going now," he said. "What about your people?"

"They've told them—it's all right. Know better than to fuss for nothing. I say, wait a min. I must tell you—daftest idea I had, when I was hit." Beddoes paused, and looked at the foot of the bed. "I thought it was a war starting—someone delivering a ballistic missile."

Nightingale regarded him in silence for a second or two. "Did you?" he murmured, finally. "Poor old Bed!"

He took his gloves off the locker, dislodging a small card that had been lying under them. He picked it up. It was obviously intended for the hospital files.

"Good Lord!" he exclaimed, reading the only thing yet written on it. "Is your name Jonathan?"

"I didn't choose it."

"You know mine?" asked Nightingale.

"Brett," said Beddoes sourly, as if he wanted to know in what respect that was superior to his own.

"That's the second one really."

"I remember—D.B.A.N., seen those initials times enough. What's the D? Oh, boil me! I'm going to laugh—I can't—my head'll split—" Beddoes' amusement was squeezed out in anguished semi-groans, he held his hands to his head.

"Goodbye," said Nightingale penitently. "I'm a disturbing influence. I'm sorry. But I quite agree. It's just a shade better to be referred to in combination as Night and Bed."

He saw as he walked away that the hands of the clock on the wall stood at five to midnight.

Part Two

Mr. Majendie's office, at which Nightingale presented himself the following morning, was a small and not too tidy room, the dead end of a corridor at the back of the premises. Nightingale imagined that Majendie had occupied these rather cramped quarters when he was a junior partner, and had adhered to them from habit or affection. No doubt he also intended their pokiness and old-fashioned furniture to correct any sense of awe or caution which might have been instilled in visitors passing through the impressive shop. This room seemed to establish that the firm, although it dealt in such exotic and sumptuous commerce, was at heart an intimate family business, in which prevailed the highest standards of integrity, courtesy and personal service; that here affairs were conducted in the spirit of a more generous age, even perhaps in a slight, homely muddle. And ensconcing himself in this little den, Majendie added another stroke to the delineation of his official character—the hamster scuffling in a nest of papers. Nightingale thought how amusing it would be to introduce a real hamster into the room and let it get to work at tearing up and stuffing into its bulging pouches all Majendie's correspondence.

"Ah, Mr. Nightingale," said Mr. Majendie, smiling cherubically. "Good morning—you know, it seems to me that in shortening our matutinal greeting we have improved in the earlier form. 'Give you good morning' on a day like this, for example, would be a superfluous, meaningless wish. Glorious weather. Whereas 'Good morning' is an enthusiastic affirmation of fact. I suppose in the case of bad weather 'Give you good morning' expresses a pious hope—but it would be more practical to substitute 'us' for 'you', a sort of mutual commiseration being thereby implanted in the petition—"

"In this country," said Nightingale, keeping his patience with an effort, "it might be as well to leave out weather conditions and let the greeting mean a wish for a good morning's work."

"Very sensible, my dear sir. Shall we to business?" He lifted a sheet of paper from under a small baboon carved in a smoky semi-opaque stone. Nightingale's eye passed from this engaging object to a book which lay near it. He felt a little surprise. 'Common Law for the Common Man' was not a title he would have expected to commend itself to Majendie.

"The list you wanted to see," said Mr. Majendie. "Mrs. Millett, my secretary, typed a new one. My own contained a good deal of technical detail which I judged less useful, for the purposes of recognition, than a more general description. I've omitted carat marks, weight, and so on, and you'll see that in the case of some of the hard-stones and other materials whose names must be unfamiliar to a layman, I've added the colour. Rhodonite, for example—"

"Pink or red?" hazarded Nightingale.

"Ah, Mr. Nightingale, but permit me to doubt whether every constable in the Metropolitan Area has the elements of Greek. And what of obsidian and bowenite—not to mention the mutations made possible by the capacity of chalcedony for staining?"

That, thought Nightingale, would perhaps teach him not to show off. Constable. *Elements* of Greek. He ought to have remembered that Majendie had been sharpening his tongue for at least a quarter-century longer than he had.

"And here," continued Mr. Majendie, "is my original list—so that you may compare them," he ended, with an unmistakable twinkle of his eyes.

Nightingale couldn't but smile back at this. He looked at the lists. They were beautifully neat, quite belying the mild confusion of their place of origin, and divided into sections, each classified. *Parure of necklace, earrings, bracelets, in square cut and brilliant diamonds (Brazilian) and square cut emeralds (Siberian), gold set.* Was that the wedding anniversary gift of Prince Sevastyan? *Rivière*—what was that?—*of large brilliant diamonds, with earrings en suite, silver. Head ornament of brilliant and rose diamonds. Ruby, pearl and emerald brooch.* Amethyst, topaz, turquoise, sapphire, tourmaline, opal, diamond, and again diamond; pendants, clips, rings, aigrettes, tiaras; the names of gems and every variety of ornament flashed in his imagination as he read. *Gold cigarette box, sunray rib, cabochon sapphire thumb piece, 3½ in., mark H.W. Gold box, engine-turned, enamelled translucent royal blue and white, rose diamond trellis, coloured gold mounts, 6 in., mark M.P. Siberian jade cigarette case, yellow gold mounts, hinges set cabochon rubies and rose diamonds, 3¼ in., mark H.W.*

"What are all these marks?" he asked, somewhat subdued.

"H.W. and M.P.? The workmaster's initials. Henrik Wigstrom and Michael Perchin, in those cases. There are others."

"Ah, Wigstrom—the one you studied with."

Mr. Majendie said nothing, but he looked so pleased that Nightingale was touched. Perhaps he was unused to having a morsel of his babble retained. Nightingale returned to the fascinating paper. Of boxes and cigarette cases alone the Princess seemed to have kept enough in her scruffy room to stock a small shop; without counting seals, sealing wax holders, scent flacons, fans, miniature frames and other objects which his eye saw in a confused jumble.

"What made her bring these small things?" he asked. "Sentimental attachment?"

"Far from it, my dear sir! Apart from the jewellery, everything on that list is made from or with gold. That was what the Princess was concerned for—saving the most valuable. Could she have foreseen the present trend of values—I wonder, should I say, of fashion?—she would have brought with her works by Fabergé in semi-precious materials, of which there were many in the Karukhin palace—some of these parasol handles, for one example, which I mentioned last night."

"It isn't all Fabergé, is it," said Nightingale. "What's this— *Louis XV oval gold box, gem-set, enamelled*—"

"Oh yes—several most interesting antiques, and among the jewellery also, though to a lesser extent, as fashion decreed that most old jewels should be refashioned from time to time. A few family pieces seem to have survived, however. Let me show you—yes, here, you see. *Late eighteenth century floral spray, pavé rose diamonds, silver set.* And here—these earrings. Also the enamelled watch, a very fine piece."

Nightingale nodded. "And a record of Jean de Reszke! May I see the letters sent to you by the Princess, please?"

"Certainly—I have them ready, but I fear I should have forgotten—Please keep them, if they will be of use to you."

"Thank you," said Nightingale, resignedly watching Majendie's plump fingerpads impressing themselves on the letters in a dozen places. He wondered whether Majendie had observed that his visitor hadn't removed his gloves. He glanced rapidly at the letters, little more than notes. "French!" he exclaimed.

"The Princess always addressed me in French—whether originally to spare her ears or my tongue I don't know."

"So you told me. But it was a point she might be excused forgetting."

"Quite so—but she didn't forget. Amazing, wasn't it? And her command of French, as you will see, appears little impaired by years of disuse. A remarkable mind."

"Yes." Nightingale slipped the papers into his wallet. As he folded the list of items, he glanced again at Majendie's valuation. It seemed to him a little on the conservative side, for such a collection; but he remembered the rhodonite, and passed no comment. What would a Fabergé fanatic be prepared to give for a sample of his work? He couldn't believe that the Hampstead people made such elaborate plans simply to acquire some gold which could be stripped of its enamel. They had a market somewhere for objets d'art, witness the removal of the shiny china so scorned by Beddoes. That meant there might be less need to despair of results from the careful observation he had wearily set in train last night. Objets d'art for a special market might still be stored somewhere in the country, even in London. The jewellery he couldn't hope to save; it was probably already broken up and on its way out.

Broken up—the words released in his mind, like the harmonics of a note, the simultaneous images of Christina's cameo and Christina's Christmas present. The juxtaposition at once seemed so inevitable that he couldn't think how it had not struck him sooner.

"Do you have cameos for sale?" he asked Majendie, hardly aware of what he was doing.

"Shell?"

"What?"

"Did you mean shell cameos?"

"I'm afraid I don't know," said Nightingale humbly, as Majendie put his head to one side in an incredulous manner. "Just an ordinary cameo," he explained lamely.

"Ah yes, a shell, no doubt," said Mr. Majendie. He pulled open a drawer in his desk and took out a box. "Now this," he said, lifting the lid and removing a large ring, "is an example of a cameo agate. Cameo is the term for carving in relief on any gem or stone. Here, you see, the layers of colour aid the relief." He handed the ring to Nightingale.

It was very handsome, he thought; the gold heavy and reddish, the carved head of a Roman-looking man extremely delicate in tiny detail. "It isn't really Roman, the stone?" he asked.

"No—a Renaissance imitation of an ancient model, and the hoop early nineteenth century. But try it, Mr. Nightingale."

"Good heavens," said Nightingale hastily, "I didn't want to—I mean, I hope you don't think I'm doing more than admire this in detachment."

"My dear sir, of course not!" expostulated Mr. Majendie in shocked tones. "But do try it—after all, why not, while you have an opportunity?"

Nightingale obeyed. It fitted him well, and he liked it.

"Very fine, Mr. Nightingale, very fine," cried Mr. Majendie, as though he were applauding. "You have an excellent hand for a ring. Come, come, don't take it off. To my mind a ring on a large, well-shaped hand, especially where the fingers are long in proportion to their breadth, as yours are, a suitable ring, I say, is a manly ornament which emphasises the strength of the hand."

That was all very flattering, Nightingale thought. On imagining the stare with which Beddoes would greet the flaunting of a ring, he grew hot. What was that other coloured stone on Majendie's list? Purpurin. It was an apt material, he felt, with which to compare the present state of his complexion. He handed back the ring.

"But you were saying," said Majendie, "that you were interested in shell cameos."

Nightingale was silent. He had not said so; but, unguardedly, he had implied it, thereby putting himself in a delicate position. If Majendie were to be implicated in the affair he was investigating, then he should have nothing to do with him in any unofficial capacity, least of all in a money transaction. Majendie, in fact, was already implicated, even if innocently. But there remained less than two days in which to buy the present, and he was now determined that it should be a cameo brooch. He couldn't be sure when or if he would be free to buy it. To defer the giving till a later date would be to disappoint her. Nobody here knew who he was or why he had come, except Majendie; and he wasn't likely to broadcast the news.

"Yes," he said, "I am. I want to buy one that's set as a brooch."

"We have a number, I believe. All at second hand, you realise? That doesn't matter? Well then, if you would care to come into the shop—I myself, I fear, have to go out in a few moments—but I'll entrust you to the care of Mr. Emmanuel."

Mr. Majendie, leaving the ring on his desk with what seemed to Nightingale foolhardy carelessness, ushered him out of the door, along the corridor past increasingly imposing offices, and into the beautiful, churchlike shop. He bounced gently towards a dark well-groomed man.

"Ah, Mr. Emmanuel," he murmured, "here is Mr. Nightingale, wishing to see some shell cameo brooches." He turned to Nightingale. "You will excuse me, my dear sir? At your service, you know, if you should want further assistance."

Beaming in a vague, all inclusive way, Mr. Majendie moved off like an old puffer train, leaving Nightingale in the hands of Mr. Emmanuel.

They were very capable hands. In a matter of seconds they had laid on top of a display case a tray of cameo brooches for him to inspect. He disregarded any that were elaborately framed, since Christina had admired her mother's for its plain encircling band of gold. But those of the collection which satisfied the condition were not the most handsome. He looked up, about to ask if there were others to be offered, and saw that a young girl had come noiselessly to Mr. Emmanuel's side. Nightingale recognised her at once; she was the girl with blonde hair, who sat on the bomb site in the sunshine, who was the youngest member of the staff; the junior odd job girl; Miss Cole.

She was murmuring a message to Mr. Emmanuel, of which Nightingale caught only the words "phone", "lapis columns" and "Louis." Mr. Emmanuel looked perturbed. With deference he begged to be excused for a few minutes.

Brett was not in the least displeased to be left with Miss Cole. He had often thought, on seeing her from a distance, that she promised to reward closer inspection, although he was not sufficiently interested to go out of his way to make it. Given this opportunity, he saw with satisfaction not only that his guess was confirmed but that she exceeded expectation. She could hardly be called pretty. Her cheekbones were very broad and high, and seemed to push her grey-green eyes upwards at the outer corners. Her eyebrows, dark as the hair of her head was fair, followed the same sharply slanting line. Her nose was short and high-bridged, her mouth wide, with the upper lip much thinner than the lower. Had the face been dull or lethargic it would have been plain; but it was suffused by a vitality so bright as to blend its somewhat uneven features into a striking whole. Everything about her proclaimed youth and health; her downy skin, the straightness of her back, the liveliness of all her movements. Brett put her age at not more than seventeen.

He couldn't fail to observe, however, that at the moment her expression seemed resentful and suspicious. She stood quite still, her hands resting on the edge of the case. She didn't meet his eyes, didn't so much as glance in his direction. She looked, in fact, as if she begrudged having to serve him.

"What I want," said Brett, "is one about this size, but with a plain rim, and not carved simply with a head. The one I want to replace was of two women dancing. Show me some like that, if you have them."

Her face seemed to darken even further. For a couple of seconds she didn't move; so that Brett was on the point of saying something quite sharply; then with a swiftness that belied her sulky face she turned to an elegant cabinet, opened its door, and slipped out a small tray, from which she picked one brooch. She held it out to Brett without a word.

He gathered himself for a concise sarcasm on the range of selection available; then stopped it. Her hand was shaking. He took the brooch without hurrying, looking at her. From time to time she folded her lips tightly, causing a tiny commotion in each cheek. It occurred to Brett that the pinkness of those cheeks might not altogether be due to well-being. He had glanced up from the cameos too often and too noticeably, and she was discomposed. At once her whole demeanour was presented in a new light. Her apparent scowl was due simply to the line of her eyebrows. She was young, the uttermost junior; and very nervous.

"Thank you," he said, and looked down at the brooch.

The design swirled across the length of the oval. Diana, slung with bow and quiver, drove her chariot through the vast expanse of sky. The legs of the team curved out in a gallop, their necks were arched, their manes flying. The goddess leaned back, her banded curls and semi-transparent draperies streaming behind her. Below and behind sailed a solitary star. The sweep of the design at first took all Brett's attention; but in detail also it was very fine. The goddess's features were quite distinct, and decidedly chaste and fair.

"You like that one?" The voice of Mr. Emmanuel spoke beside him.

"Yes," said Brett, looking up with a start. He laid the brooch on the case.

"It is a fine example of carving," said Mr. Emmanuel, taking it up. "Good shell, too. Well fitted to the subject. That dark greyish colour is right for the night sky. A lot of them would be too brown."

He held it to the light to demonstrate how thin it was, and the carving appeared in reverse like black tracery. Brett shivered. Christina must not be allowed to leave this one on the piano.

"No frame, of course," went on Mr. Emmanuel.

"What's that, then?"

"Well, that just holds it and supports the pin, really. Compare it with this." Mr. Emmanuel pointed out a monstrous circle of chased yellow gold which seemed to crush the central cameo inwards.

"That's exactly what I didn't want," said Brett. He smiled at Miss Cole, to let both her and Mr. Emmanuel know where he bestowed credit for the satisfaction of his wishes; but she was looking away from him. He drew out his cheque book. "How much?" he asked, writing the date.

"Fifteen pounds," said Mr. Emmanuel, after the tiniest pause. "You've less gold to pay for than people who prefer more substantial frames. Shall we parcel it for you?" he concluded, with a little edge to his voice.

"Yes," said Brett, smothering an over emphatic *of course*. Mr. Emmanuel's trained eye must have seen that his pen hovered an instant too long before descending again on the cheque. Quickly he wrote Majendie's name, the price, his signature and his address on the back. The cheque passed into Mr. Emmanuel's discreet hand. In return he received an almost weightless package neatly wrapped by Miss Cole. The transaction was made.

Forcing himself to shake off a certain uneasiness, Brett thanked the girl. For once, she was looking straight at him; and, he felt, with some curiosity. He smiled determinedly, to see if he could not break her seriousness. But at that moment Mr. Emmanuel waved her away.

"Fine weather," he observed, handing the cheque to a passing assistant with a look that urged him to despatch. "I shall be surprised if it holds, though. When that sky covers we'll have to look out for snow. White Christmas, if we're lucky."

"Yes," said Brett without enthusiasm. He was in no mood to be entertained by post-sales talk. Miss Cole had disappeared.

He had done something which he was cross with himself for half regretting.

He stared gloomily across the shop. Through an arch he could see into another room, where three men were discussing some porcelain bowls which lay before them, and which at frequent intervals they lifted and tapped with their knuckles. The bowls gave forth pure, bell-like notes. Sometimes two were struck in quick succession, and the rooms throbbed to mellow tones or semitones. *Ring out, ye crystall sphears, Once bless our human ears,* thought Brett. This was the month, after all, and nearly the happy morn. And he could think of something else he'd like once to bless his ears. No information had greeted him this morning, no encouraging reports of unusual underworld activity, no dank Ivan fished from the canal. He hadn't yet spoken to the Division; they, perhaps, would have unearthed a little of what he'd asked about, although they hadn't had much time for probing.

With relief he took his receipt, managed a civil farewell to Mr. Emmanuel, and departed for a less luxurious sphere of operations.

———

Outside the divisional office he met Beddoes.

"I left early," said he hastily, while Nightingale was still staring at him in silence. "I am all right. I told you I was last night. No one tried to stop me coming out, anyway."

"No, I suppose you'll pass," said Nightingale, looking him up and down. "How's the head?"

"Functioning quite normally, I think, thanks. Were you going in to see what they've got for you?"

"Yes. But as you've been before me I needn't bother—I hope?"

Beddoes shook his head, and then flinched. "I'll tell you. Where shall we go?"

"I'll drive down to the car park and we can sit there in the car. I've a flask of coffee—you can have some if you like, but it's black and sweetened and there's only the flask cup to share with me."

Beddoes was already making a face and noise such as small children often make when served with a helping of spinach.

"Good," said Nightingale, "I can have it all. There wasn't going to be much for two. Anyway, I expect it would have been bad for you."

As he drove down the road he outlined his gleanings from Majendie. Beddoes received with his usual affectation of non-chalance the description of some of Princess Olga's treasures; and Majendie's valuation with a gesture of scepticism.

"So I thought," said Nightingale. "Even if he's nothing worse, I think he was prepared to slice the Princess. As she was a half deranged recluse he may have valued them even lower for her than he'd dare do for us. But I don't know—she wasn't that mad. Anyway, he and his partners must have been fairly rubbing their hands in anticipation of the profits."

"Of course," said Beddoes, "as far as Majendie knows, Ivan Karukhin is the legitimate heir, and there'd be nothing to stop him selling if the lot was recovered. So he doesn't want to risk admitting the real value even now."

"Still hoping to pull off the deal, yes. He did his best to lead me to expect a low price last night—*after* he'd discovered which way the wind was blowing. What he'd first described as a considerable purchase suffered a metamorphosis, ended as a considerable risk."

Nightingale backed the car into a space between two others, pulled his flask out of the pocket and unscrewed the top. "Tell me," he began, leaning over the side of the car to pour in safety, "—just a minute, do you find it too cold? I didn't put up the hood, it's such a lovely day. There's a rug in the boot, if you'd like it."

"No thank you," said Beddoes patiently. "One minor mishap hasn't undermined my health. Well, they didn't get much more about Ivan from St. Pancreas—"

"You'll say that when you're giving evidence one day, you know."

"Dull but inoffensive, it seems. Went there straight from school at fourteen, recommended by old headmaster. How anyone could recommend Ivan I don't know. However, they took him as office boy. Lucky to get that, in those times, in view of his qualifications, or lack. Couldn't be used for portering, not strong enough. He was often off sick as it was. Sometimes they sent him home when his asthma got too bad. Never a sign of drunkenness at work, so if he soaked regularly as much as I saw him do last night he must have been able to sleep it off something stunning. Station people could hardly find a thing to say about him, apparently. They sound tolerant, but I think they'd really almost forgotten him. He did very minor clerical work, no set groove, just here and there as needed. No complaints of the way he did it. I don't suppose they'll miss him. Odd though, he was all over the place on the twenty-second, and quite talkative."

"Not at all odd. He overacted, that's all. Have they found his old school?"

"Yes, it was the one nearest Bright's Row. They went there first, only this morning. Or rather, they asked the head direct, as they know him well. But he didn't remember Ivan personally, he looked him up on the old registers. Ivan's forty, don't forget. The head who recommended him retired some years ago. He's still alive though, and they got his address. Esher. Someone's gone."

"Good. What about pubs?"

"Ripe," said Beddoes, "very ripe. The local boys knew his favourite. Not the one where I met him. The Oak Tree. Landlord's all right, very informative. It seems Ivan's known as Prince—he sometimes used to protest his noble birth when he'd had a few, and the regulars used to egg him on for their own harmless diversion. He'd also taken to boasting of what he'd do when he came into his inheritance, alternatively, making vague allegations that he'd been maliciously deprived of same. No one ever took Ivan seriously, according to the landlord. The divi asked him if he ever had shady birds in the pub. He said they nearly all looked shady to him, and some were proper pitch. Instanced Sowman and Pomphilion— quite upset when the divi wasn't impressed. But then he said he'd served Stan Wacey."

Nightingale raised his eyebrows. "Someone saw him in Vanbrugh Street the other day. What's he doing here?"

"He lives round here, don't you remember?"

"Lord, I'm corrupt! I can't think of people like Wacey going into a pub just because it's their local and they want a drink, I must start looking for what they're after. But he's behaving, isn't he? He's not long out. When was he first in the Oak Tree, do you know?"

"A couple of months ago. And he hasn't been there since."

"It may not mean a thing, of course. Wacey couldn't have been connected with Hampstead, at least, for the good reason of being inside at the time. Nor may Ivan have done more than look at him, though he could have included him in one of his apparently habitual un-bosomings about his—"

Nightingale stopped. His inheritance. His Fabergé. Part of Beddoes' report of last night suddenly burst into flames of significance.

"What do you take Ivan's talk of an egg to mean?" he asked.

"Ivan was bats," said Beddoes gloomily.

"I don't think so. I mean, not necessarily in that respect. I've told you what's on Majendie's list. Fabergé. Fabergé and eggs, Beddoes—"

"Wait a min! I've heard of those. Easter Eggs made of gold and diamonds and what you will, with little surprises inside in the same style. But weren't they all for the Tsar to give to the Tsaritsa or his mother?"

"I believe anyone who could afford could have one, and God knows, the Karukhins were wealthy enough. Suppose there was an egg like ice and frost and stars?"

"Not on Majendie's list, is it?"

"No. But it would be too outstanding, surely, to miss or forget."

"Maybe the old girl got rid of it, or didn't show it because she didn't want to part with it. Maybe it didn't exist except in Ivan's disordered brain."

"Perhaps. I must get hold of one or all of Majendie's partners on the side, and see whether they really were told of an impending Karukhin deal. I could hardly ask him to bring them to me this morning and then tell him to leave us—well, not without proclaiming how suspicious he seems to me. And now we have to think of Wacey, possibly an unwitting red herring, but we'll scout him out, all the same. And look here—the landlord said no one took Ivan seriously. Why should Wacey, if he heard him?"

"Principle of no stone unturned when there might be lolly under it."

"Possibly. But don't you think it is rather remarkable that he should appear at that particular pub? I know you said he lives there, but—"

"You think he was planted?"

"Someone could have overheard one of Ivan's earlier outbursts—someone with enough interest to prick up their ears at any mention of an inheritance, even a drunk's. Someone with enough general knowledge to realise that the name Karukhin—oh, they could have *asked*, Beddoes!—was a promising one, promising because it's Russian, and Russians have sometimes owned valuable property of a particularly thief-worthy sort. They needn't have had particular knowledge of the Karukhin family."

"This someone, you'd like to think, being in with the Hampstead people, being one of them, perhaps?"

"Why not? And when Wacey came out and picked up with them, he was the chosen instrument, being local, for the case."

Beddoes was thoughtful. "Well, we know who'd prick up his ears at the name, if only because he'd had a taste in the twenties and could very well guess that more of the family possessions he'd known in Petersburg had come over than just the diamond and ruby brooch."

"Oh Lord! Yes."

"Why oh Lord?"

"Nothing. Anyway, there's Ivan. Whoever *isn't* involved, he is."

"If he knew grandma was in the potential lolly and wouldn't hand out, I suppose that accounts for the Russian rows Mrs. Minelli heard."

"That reminds me, I must have a word with her this evening. And I forgot to tell you that the Princess wanted the proceeds of the sale to go direct to a school for the daughters of the nobility."

"Boil me!" said Beddoes wearily.

Nightingale started the engine. Beddoes' almost complete lack of effervescence had been nowhere more marked than in his reception of that piece of information.

"Where are we going?" he asked now.

"There's something I want you to do," said Nightingale. Out of the corner of his eye he saw Beddoes sit up straight and try to look attentive. "I'm afraid you'll have do this my way. No deviation, none of your own ideas, and strict adherence to orders." Beddoes had turned on him a stare of disbelieving reproach. "You're to go home to bed," said Nightingale calmly, "and not show your face to me till tomorrow morning."

"All right," said Beddoes.

"Mind now, no evasion," warned Nightingale, suspicious of such prompt and unqualified submission. "There's no point in making a martyr of yourself. Remember what you said when the A.C. would persist in coming in when he had that foul cold. You didn't know I'd overheard that, did you? I've been saving it in the hope that I could use it on such an occasion as this. You said—"

"But he was spreading germs!"

"You said that when people were so groggy they could only crawl about like cold flies in a coma they'd do better to stay in bed. You're not that bad yet, but you will be if you don't do as I say. I'll take you to Charing Cross—that's where you go from, isn't it? All right. And on the way I'll give you a history lesson—the history of a princely family. I learnt it last night while you were paddling the canal."

Having ejected Beddoes into the station, he left the car in the forecourt and walked through to the reference library in

St. Martin Street; where he was soon engrossed by a hand-some book describing and lavishly illustrating the art of Carl Fabergé.

It was only as he left the library an hour or so later that he discovered the loss of one glove.

———

Brett glanced again at the note lying on top of the refrigerator. However slight and informal the message, Christina never scribbled, never failed to address it to dear Brett. *Dear Brett—* Ticket here if you want to come on. Sorry not to wait, but I want to see T. in interval to secure promise of introduction to S. afterwards. Your clothes have come. Please try for fit tonight so that they can be sent back for alteration, if necessary, in good time. They're on the bed. And this came second post from Henry. Christina.

He stared at the three kisses with which she had orna-mented the note; she must have been feeling very expansive, or very hilarious, or both, to have thrown those in. His eye travelled from them to the clear rural post mark on the enve-lope that had held his brother's record token; thence to the green stripes of the ticket. Neither of them would have stirred a foot to hear the concert if it hadn't been conducted by some-one whose acquaintance Christina considered desirable. He still had time—for what? To sit through the undistinguished second half, then either come home without her or go to the back and be in the way. He left the ticket where it was. He looked once at the dishes he had stacked on the draining board, and left those where they were too.

He set some coffee on the stove, and went out, up the small spiral stair to the bedroom, where he switched on the light and the fire. The clothes, carefully laid out, looked rather pleasing. He began to undress, reflecting on the wilful folly, as it seemed to him, of the committee of the North-West London Opera Group, which had decreed that this year the annual performance should take place a few days after Christmas. Booking was reported to be encouraging, but he doubted whether, when the time came, more than half of the ticket holders would have strength to rise from their armchair torpor. He had seldom been so pleased, however, by the choice of opera and the part assigned to him.

His life, he thought, was taking a heavy dose of things Russian at this time; although the Karukhins were, technically, Russian no longer. He had heard from the Home Office. Olga Karukhin had applied for British nationality in September 1926, and had duly received the certificate, in which the name of her grandson, a minor, was also entered; and had duly taken the oath of allegiance. Ivan had not, on attaining majority, repudiated his status. He was British, claiming British rights, protected by British laws and justice; and subject to the same.

Brett's hopes had risen. At least four British subjects must have known the Princess well enough to vouch for her character. He'd asked for their names and addresses. All of them had been resident in Stockholm in 1926, three of them members of the Foreign Service, the fourth a doctor. They were elderly then; now they were probably dead. Yet once here she would have had to advertise her intention to become British. Surely some Russians, immigrés or émigrés, whichever way they looked on themselves, would have seen that, or have had it brought to their notice? Why hadn't they sought her out? The Princess, he remembered, had not been loved.

Brett sighed. The case had reached a point at which

nothing could be done but wait, hoping that lines already flung out would take catches. He was grateful for the lull in so far as it had permitted him to come home: its effect was nevertheless depressing after the frustrations of the afternoon. One of Majendie's partners was nursing a chill, another in New York, and the last already away for Christmas. Mrs. Minelli was all that Beddoes had said, and no more. The only morsel of interest she had to offer him was that Mrs. Karukhin's habit of locking the door was of comparatively recent growth, though she could not say exactly when it had started. Apart from this, there was no information—and no Ivan. But they were finished with the canal. Ivan was not there, at least not in that strip of it.

Ivan Ilarionovich Karukhin. The old headmaster at Esher remembered him as a sickly boy, often absent; his character as weak as his body, though in no way vicious; his mental calibre low. At fourteen he could write but not spell, and was capable of only simple reading and arithmetic. The headmaster had exerted himself on Ivan's behalf, to see him placed even in a low position, because he could not help pitying so timorous, lonely and neglected a boy, dressed always in other children's ill-fitting cast-offs, whose only relative was the old grandmother who had never stirred from their room since Ivan started school, and who had imposed on him from the age of six the entire task of shopping.

All in all, Brett was not surprised that the pathologists, communicating the first results of their examination just before he left the office had cautiously concluded that appearances were not so far inconsistent with barbiturate poisoning. The cocoa in the mugs was still with the analysts; but Brett didn't feel he had to wait on what they might tell him. One of his lines was cast to find out whether, when, where, or how

Ivan had acquired sleeping tablets. That would take time, unless his stupidity had made it easy for them. Brett didn't care how long it took. As far as he was concerned, the death of Olga Vassilievna was an incident in the course of a case already begun; nor, as far as he could see, was it the sort of incident which, followed to the last detail, would help him to settle any more quickly his score with the Hampstead people. Olga Vassilievna, Princess Karukhin—there was a parallel, he thought, with *The Queen of Spades*. An old Russian aristocrat, dead in her bedroom for the sake of a profitable secret.

He surveyed himself in the mirror. The costume wasn't at all bad. He added the hat, and was prepared to twirl into some of his prescribed antics, when the door bell rang.

He hesitated for a second or two, conscious of his some-what ludicrous appearance; then he went out and down the stairs. If the caller were a friend it wouldn't matter what sort of figure he cut, and if it were a stranger it would matter still less. He didn't think it could be anyone who knew them well, because the ring had come from the lower door, although he remembered that it was open and the stairs lit. He crossed the hall, opened the door and looked down the flight.

He was so taken aback by what he saw that for a moment he couldn't put a name to the girl, although he recognised her. He knew he had seen her recently, but not where.

"Good evening," he called. "Won't you come up?"

She shot a swift glance up the stairs.

"Of course!" he murmured. She was Miss Cole, the girl from Majendie's.

"Good evening," he repeated as she arrived at the top. He tried to sound less puzzled than he felt.

"Good evening." The words were muttered so rapidly as to be almost inaudible. With what seemed to be great reluctance she raised her eyes; whereupon her diffident frown lightened into a fixed stare of astonishment.

"Sorry about these," said Brett, recalling that she was receiving her first full view of the costume. "I was trying them. Come in." He closed the door behind her, and turned round.

"The thing is," she said quickly, before he had time even to look inquiring, "you dropped a glove in the shop this morning, and I've brought it back to you."

He was at once enlightened and more perplexed.

"Yes," she went on, at the same speed, "I found it on the floor by the case. It must have got pushed off the top by the tray while you were looking at the cameos. Or else you knocked it down without noticing while you were writing the cheque. Anyway—"

She opened her handbag, fumbling a little, and took out the glove, which, old and rubbed as it was, had been wrapped in a sheet of paper tissue.

"Thank you," said Brett, taking it, and stifling a wish to laugh. Majendie's carried their personal service to outrageous lengths. "Did you—"

He broke off. A strong smell of coffee had reached his nose.

"Good Lord! I forgot," he exclaimed. "Excuse me—" He dashed into the kitchen. The coffee was in no danger, only bubbling rather frantically. He lowered the heat, and went back to the hall.

She was standing just where he had left her. Her eyes, darting apparently habitual nervous sulks, were even brighter than they had appeared in the shop, and her cheeks were rosier; probably, Brett thought, on account of the cold.

"I was making coffee," he said. "You'll stay for some?"

"Please don't trouble—"

"There's no trouble," he said. "In fact, I didn't even have to make it. My wife left it ready for me. Please stay, if you've time."

"All right. Yes, I've got time," she said awkwardly. "Thank you very much."

"Good." Brett opened the living-room door and switched on the light. "There's a fire in here—it should blaze up if I poke it about a bit."

Having removed the guard, altered the damper, pulled an armchair closer to the fire, taken her coat and seen her comfortably settled, he went outside and permitted himself a quiet grin of congratulation. The evening had taken a pleasant turn, thanks to his inspired impulse with regard to the coffee.

He hung up her coat, which was soft, warm, and pale pink. A coat of that quality, he reflected, would cost her at least a month's wages. He looked at the label, and nodded. Majendie's junior must be only nominally independent of indulgent parents. His eye was caught by a name, professionally embroidered on the silk lining. Stephanie Cole. Stephanie.

Still smiling, Brett went into the kitchen and started to set a tray at high speed. He warmed some milk, in case she didn't like cream; and mindful of a certain sleek plumpness about her figure, which was kept trim, he suspected, by exercise rather than regulation of diet, he put out a plate of biscuits. He caught sight of the concert ticket on top of the refrigerator, and his smile grew a shade scornful.

When, a few minutes later, he edged through the living-room door with the tray, she stood up quickly.

"Can I do anything?" she asked.

"Yes, please," said Brett. "Clear a space on the small table and pull it close to your chair."

He stood watching her. She was dressed as for a party, in

a crisp black silk skirt and a scoop-necked blouse knitted in black wool that sparkled. A gold locket hung from a chain round her neck. Had her hair been braided, as at Majendie's, the total effect would have been rather too severe; but it was drawn back through a ring clip and left to hang in a straight switch or tail almost to her waist.

She looked up.

"I think I should hardly have known you this evening," he said, quickly. "After the plaits, the grey dress—"

"Long hair gets untidy at work. And everyone has to wear that grey, at least, the women. A sort of uniform."

"It's the dress of a stage Puritan," he said, setting down the tray.

At last, suddenly, she smiled; a cheek-rippling, utterly minx-like smile, accompanied by a downcast glance.

Somewhat thoughtfully, Brett indicated the cream jug, and she nodded. "I hope," he said, pouring the coffee with care, "you didn't have too cold a journey. Did you have far to come?"

"Sanderstead."

"What?" Brett nearly dropped the pot. "Do you mean to tell me there's no one at Majendie's who lives on this side of London to have brought me an old dropped glove?"

She was silent, blushing slightly, and showing a trace of her resentful look. It occurred to Brett that Majendie's had sacrificed to their punctilio the person least in a position to protest.

"But surely," he went on, "they meant you to come here from Fitch Street?"

"Majendie's didn't send me," she said, "I came by myself."

"Oh," said Brett, and handed her the cup. His head filled with pelting queries, which he decided for the present to ignore.

"Are you an actor?" she asked, tipping a heaped spoonful of sugar into her cup.

He hesitated. He didn't want to explain the reason for his outlandish garments; yet not to do so would be too pointed a snub of a purely natural question. "No," he said, "I belong to an amateur opera club."

She didn't seem unduly surprised. "What opera are you doing, and what part have you got?" she asked.

"*Love for Three Oranges*. I'm Truffaldino." He paused, in two minds whether or not further information would be necessary or acceptable.

"Love for Three Oranges," she repeated. "That's Russian, isn't it? Prokofiev? Oh, it just happens to be something I've heard Geoffrey talk about. He works in Kellett's," she explained, "the gramophone shop, you know. He quite often has lunch with me."

"Does he work in the front of the shop, selling?"

"Yes."

"In his middle twenties, one eye blue and the other brown?"

Stephanie stared. "How *did* you guess?"

"He looks like a Geoffrey." It was a name Brett particularly disliked. He recalled the young man as a supercilious weed with a wrung-out voice.

"Oh," said Stephanie, rather uncertainly. "Of course, he knows everything there is to know about music. He's rather a bore, actually. Not because of what he talks about," she added quickly, "but because of the way he says it. All the time I feel he's preaching—no, not that exactly. Thinking he's awfully good to teach me."

"Patronising," suggested Brett, guiltily recollecting his own attitude to her probable knowledge of *Love for Three Oranges*. "Condescending."

"Yes," she said, "I can never think of the right word. Of course, he's not too bad. Anyway it's awfully hard to avoid talking to people once they've actually sat down beside you and said hullo."

"Try going somewhere else for lunch!" said Brett.

"What, and waste my luncheon vouchers? I shouldn't have much left after I'd paid my fares."

Brett nodded. A certain edge to her lively voice reminded him of Beddoes; and there was a similarity of accent; no doubt, a coincidence, although Beddoes lived not far from Sanderstead.

"You like working at Majendie's?" he asked.

"Oh, it's all right. Rather boring—at least, for me. Tidying the office cupboards, typing address labels—two fingers, I can't really type—just doing any odd thing that nobody else can be bothered with. I wouldn't mind if I could have more to do with the things in the shop. They're lovely, some of them. But the only time I get a look is when I have to help the packers or dust the cases. Or get something out of the window for Mr Lowrie, he's so fat."

"I don't see what more you could have to do with them," said Brett, "short of selling them to other people, in which case you wouldn't see them for long. After all, I doubt whether even Mr. Majendie sits in front of a piece of porcelain in rapt contemplation."

"He does, you know," said Stephanie. "I've seen him in his little office, when the door's been open, sitting staring at something on his desk—not porcelain, usually jewellery. You can see he's quite gone. I don't know how he can bear to part with—all that."

"Perhaps he doesn't," said Brett. "I suppose it wouldn't be too difficult for him to hang on to something he particularly fancied." He reflected that Majendie's house, though far from sparsely furnished, had not struck him as being overstocked with obvious collector's pieces. But if, in his own words, and as Stephanie confirmed, jewellery was his great love, he could have a massive collection that was not displayed.

"He has a collection," said Stephanie, causing Brett to jump at the echo of his thought, "down in Kent. It's rather odd, that. His house isn't far from my aunt's farm. Only how I found out was when I was helping Mrs. Millet, his secretary to tidy one of the cupboards in his room. She went out, and he came in, and started talking away to me. He's awfully sweet, you know. He asked me what I was doing at Christmas—this was only the other morning—and I told him we always went down to this farm at Pettinge. 'Pettinge, near Folkestone?' he said. 'But that's only a few miles from my own home. You know Barton, Miss Cole?' and so on, and so on. He said I must call during the holiday and he'd show me his collection, said it would be interesting and useful to me. But I don't suppose he really meant it."

"Don't you?" said Brett. "I do. I think he really wants you to learn." He didn't say what else he was thinking, that if Stephanie had been less attractive the offer would never have been made. "You're not unseen down among the cases and cupboards, and you won't always stay there. By the way, what is a Chaffers?"

"A big fat reference book of marks on porcelain. Why?"

"Nothing. After all, they have to watch you for a while, to make sure you're not completely dense or butterfingered, before they let you—"

"Oh, don't, don't!" she interrupted impatiently. "I've had all that from Daddy. Probation, work your way up, learning the ropes, Rome not built in a day, et cetera. I suppose by the time I'm an old crow of forty they might let me into the holy of holies."

"More coffee?" asked Brett.

"No, thank you. It was awfully nice coffee, though." She put her cup on the tray, and her eyes rested, not for the first time, on the photograph of Christina which stood inconspicuously enough on the bookcase. "Is that your wife?"

"A photograph of her," said Brett, idiotically.

She shot him a well-merited look. "Is she English?"

"Yes."

She shook her head. "So dark!"

"She doesn't look exactly like that now," Brett volunteered. "She had her hair cut short a few weeks ago."

"What a shame! It suits her in that bun."

"I'm sorry you haven't met her," said Brett. "She's gone to hear the new cantata. Has Geoffrey mentioned it?"

"If he has, I wasn't listening. Didn't you want to go too?"

"I was going, but I came home too late."

She looked at him in frank curiosity. "What's your work?"

"Guess!"

"That's just the trouble," she complained, "I can't. Does your wife work too?"

"She's a singer."

"Good heavens! What sort of singer?"

"Chiefly of opera. She's a mezzo-soprano. You can ask Geoffrey if he's heard of Christina Gallen, but he may not know her. She was in Germany till this summer, and she hasn't sung here since she came home, just taken a rest and looked about her. But I think she's getting tired of doing nothing."

He wished ardently that Christina were at home. She was adept at the sweet dispatch of lingering visitors. Pleasant as it was to talk and listen to Stephanie, he had to consider the length of her journey home and the fact that it was already quite late.

"Do you go from Victoria?" he asked, crudely.

She looked reluctantly at the clock. "As a matter of fact I came to Charing Cross," she said.

"Tattenham Corner line, and change. All right. I'll bring the car round."

"Oh no—please don't bother," she said, embarrassed. "I came on the tube to Camden Town. It's only a little way."

"Not so little. And why walk?"

"But you mustn't," she protested, not very convincingly. He ignored this, and went out to the hall. As he lifted her coat from the peg he saw his glove lying on the table. Thoughtfully he picked it up.

"Are you going out like that?"

He turned round. She had followed him out of the room, and was regarding him with an air of incredulous delight. He became aware of his gaudy Truffaldino clothes.

"No one will see," he said, holding the coat for her, not too close to him, but on the other hand not too far away.

"But won't you be cold?" She slipped her arms into the sleeves, and raised a hand to flick her hair free of the collar; not quite succeeding, so that a few strands clung like cobwebs to the downy material and straggled in an untidy loop across her shoulder. Brett managed to resist the temptation to set this to rights. Her hair was very pretty, evenly fair, glittering in its cleanness. There was no wave to it, as there had been in Christina's when she let it down. The switch hung straight, marked only by the tiny kinks which constant plaiting imparts.

Brett rather absently unhooked a thick shapeless cardigan and put it on, following it by his coat. "At least," he said, "I have my glove now." He held it on the palm of his hand. "How did you do it?"

"What?" she parried.

"Get hold of it, know it was mine, find out where to bring it, everything. I'm just curious."

"I found it this morning. After you'd gone, about half an hour after, I had to dust the glass shelf in that case, Did you notice there was a patch of dust on it? No, I didn't think anyone would, except Mr. Emmanuel. Anyway I knelt down to open the back of the case and put my duster on the floor, and when I picked it up I saw the edge of the glove sticking out by the leg of the case. It must have fallen off the top and got kicked under either by me or Mr. Emmanuel. There's only about four inches between the bottom of the case and the carpet. You couldn't have seen it lying there."

"How did you know it was mine?"

"Oh well, it was obvious. I mean, I recognised it. I remembered what your gloves looked like as they lay on the case. Anyway I just knew it was yours."

"What about the address?"

"I watched you write it on the back of the cheque."

He frowned. "Upside down—"

"But you wrote in capitals. It was quite easy."

"Only for someone making a special effort to read. Were you?"

"Yes, I was, rather."

"Why?"

"I was just curious."

"But why the whole thing?" he persisted. "Why not have given this miserable glove to the lost property person, or Mr. Emmanuel? Don't Majendie's have security officers on the premises? Yes, of course. Suppose one of them had seen you whipping up this article belonging to a customer? How did you do it? Wrapped it in your duster, I imagine, and took it out to hide in your handbag. What could look more suspicious! Suppose I'd come back, swearing and insisting I'd lost the glove in the shop? How were you to know I wouldn't notice for some time that it was gone? Yes, I know it sounds implausible, but Majendie's would do anything to placate a customer who threatened to make a fuss. There are such people, and I might have been one of them. Don't you see what risks you took? And for what?" He paused. "Why *did* you do it?"

"I don't know," she said, hesitantly. "Well—suddenly it was there in front of me, and just even while I was seeing what it was, I saw I had a chance to do something—oh, different, quite exciting, really—no, not the getting the glove to the locker, that was just something that had to be done—but coming here. That is, somewhere new, where I hadn't been before."

Brett was silent. Then how was it that she'd taken such pains to read his address *before* finding the glove?

"It's so boring, usually," she added.

"What is?"

She heaved a great sigh, and leaned back against the wall. "Everything. I want—I don't know."

Brett looked at her, particularly at that long creamy curve of neck. He recalled to mind the knitted blouse at present concealed by the coat; and in that connection, one of Beddoes' succinct dicta: every neckline tells a story. He thought he knew what Stephanie wanted. Unfortunately, as she said, and with truth, he was quite sure, she didn't know herself. He reflected with a wry smile how calamitous it would be if he were so far to transgress his own law of the permissible as even to utter any of his several suggestions.

"Well, that train!" he said innocuously. "I suppose you have to work as usual tomorrow?"

"Only the morning," she said, following him to the kitchen without question. "We close at twelve-thirty, so we can all go."

He stopped. "I didn't put the guard round the fire. I think I'd better. Wait here a moment." He slipped back to the living room. As he attended to the fire, he observed that he was still wearing Truffaldino's slippers; but he couldn't be bothered with going upstairs to find a pair of shoes.

He returned to the kitchen, opened the broom cupboard, and pulled out a pair of dusty wellingtons.

"It's not wet out," said Stephanie, watching him struggle into the boots, which were stiff from disuse. "Still, they're warmer, I suppose. They're like what my uncle wears—the one on the farm."

"Are you going down tomorrow?" he asked.

"Straight from work."

"Then you'll have all your packing to do tonight," he said.

"Oh no," she said. "My parents are going on ahead in the car. Mummy takes all my things for me."

"The car," he said, remembering that he was supposed to be making for his own. "Do you mind coming down the fire escape and across the garden? It's rather dark, but much quicker, and as you say, it's not wet—"

"That's fine," she assured him.

He picked up his torch and switched it on. They went out, down the iron stairs, across the grass hardened into the likeness of an unmade road by the severe cold. The wind skewered their arms to their sides.

"You're going by train tomorrow?" asked Brett, opening the back door into the garage.

"Yes. The Man of Kent. So's Mr. Majendie."

"He doesn't drive?" Brett held the door of the car for her.

"Not all the way. He keeps his car in a lock-up at Folkestone and just takes it to and from his house. He told me all this the other morning. You know."

"When he asked you to come and see the collection," called Brett from the front of the garage.

"Do you see anything funny in that?" she asked haughtily, as he came and sat beside her.

"No, not at all," he lied.

"Oh. Good. Neither did Geoffrey. Daddy laughed for hours."

"So Geoffrey doesn't have it all his own way in the lunch-hour conversation!"

She tossed her head, causing the switch of hair to flick from side to side. Brett drove forward.

"I never thought I'd actually sit in this car," she said.

"You mean in a car of this kind?"

"No," she cried indignantly. "In this actual one."

"How did you know that I had a car?"

"I've seen you in it." She sounded surprised that he hadn't understood the obvious. "I noticed you first one day last summer. You drove down Fitch Street and went into the private recording studio. I've often seen you since. Sometimes you go in Kellett's, too. This is a new car, isn't it, though it's the same make and colour as the other. I noticed the different number plates."

"I see."

"No," she said blithely, "I did the seeing—from my little garden. The bomb site, I mean, the one next door. It's lovely and warm and sunny, and there's a lot of that pink flower—well, it's a weed really, but it's very pretty."

"Rose-bay Willow-herb. Did you know a florist's used to stand there?"

"Yes, Geoffrey told me. It's not much of a site for an individual shop, is it? No way out to the back alley and no cellars. Ours and Kellett's meet in the middle, I think. At least, ours go under an awfully long way. Yes, I think they must, because you can see the patching up they had to do when the bomb fell, and it was only a little one, they say, a fire bomb."

"And now Kellett's own the site. What on earth do they want it for? I should have thought they were big enough already."

"I know. Actually—" She hesitated, and flicked her hair rapidly. "That's one reason why I feel it would be rather off to cut Geoffrey. You see, I used to sit on that bomb site after lunch in the fine weather. It was so nice and sheltered. Then when Kellett's took over they complained to Mr. Majendie that I was trespassing."

"Rather petty. They haven't started to build even now. You wouldn't have been in the way."

"Mr. Majendie was furious, Mrs. Millet said, not with me but with Kellett's, for sending the message across so rudely. Anyway, I can't sit there any more. And you see, Geoffrey used to come back and sit there too, once or twice, so I'm sure he must have got into trouble over it, though he never said so. And it would be on my account."

He drew up at a red light and glanced at her. He saw her slide back her sleeve with one finger and look down at her watch.

"You want to catch a particular train?"

"It doesn't matter." She moved her hand guiltily.

"Do your parents know where you are?" he asked, as the car went forward.

She gave her head an extra violent toss. "I don't have to tell them everything I do. Actually, they were out," she admitted.

"And you're hoping to be home before them, so that you needn't explain that you trailed twice across London to return a glove to a strange man."

"You're not strange," she said, rather sulkily.

"How so? Not strange, and you heard me speak for the first time this morning?"

"Oh, you can tell by what people look like."

"Fatal error. You're heading for disaster."

"Well, voices—"

"Worse still. Don't you know the old song? Do not trust him, gentle maiden, Though his voice be—whatever it is."

She laughed. "How odd you should say that. Your voice isn't in the least what I expected. I thought it would be all incisive and arresting—"

"Arrest—"

"You know, commanding, and that. And instead it's all lazy and drawly. You're not American, are you?"

"No. My mother was, from the South, too."

"Ah, then that accounts for it."

"I don't see how it can. And on the other hand my father came from Yorkshire."

"Oh." She was silent for a moment or two. "Have you any children?"

"No."

"Oh. Any brothers or sisters?"

"One elder brother. And you?"

"One elder sister. That's where they've gone this evening. Usually we all go down to Pettinge, but this year she can't because the baby's too young, so they were taking over the Christmas presents."

"First baby? How old?"

"Two months."

The tone of her voice made him look sharply at her.

"You're not fond of babies?" he asked.

"They're all right, in moderation. Actually he's rather sweet. But it makes me tired, the way people go on about it."

"Who do? Your parents?"

"Yes. And everyone."

Neither of them spoke for a while.

"I love this car," said Stephanie, eventually. "You are lucky."

"Your father has a car, I think you said."

"Not what I call a car. A family saloon. Oh, boredom, boredom! Boredom ineffable!"

"There's a big word," murmured Brett, swinging into the forecourt of Charing Cross. "Poor father. That's a nice coat he bought you, all the same." He slid the car up to the kerb. "Well, I'm sorry you didn't see my wife. But perhaps it's just as well she was out. Can you think why I bought that cameo?"

"To give to her, I suppose."

"Yes, as a Christmas present. But if she'd heard you talking about Majendie's and brooches and dropped gloves she wouldn't have had much of a surprise on Christmas morning."

"I never thought," said Stephanie, looking very chastened. "I suppose it was really rather off, the whole thing. I'm sorry." She paused. "But would you mind terribly not saying anything about it to Mr. Emmanuel?"

"Why on earth should I say anything to *him*? I doubt if I'll ever speak to him again."

"I thought he must be a friend of yours," she said, surprised.

"Why?"

"Because he knocked thirty-five pounds off that cameo for you."

Brett felt as if he'd stepped down a kerb in a dozing dream and had jerked awake. "What?" he said, stupidly.

"Well, of course, I know prices are often altered for special people, so I didn't think anything of it. I only happened to know the real value because I'd been dusting the office while the consignment was sorted. That's how I knew where to look for it too. Is anything the matter?"

He shook his head.

"Are you all right?" Her voice had risen in pitch, and trembled slightly.

He heard the unmistakable note of alarm, and pulled himself together. He must look as ghastly as he felt, and he had always condemned people who in their full age plucked the nerves of the impressionable young by uncontrolled displays of emotional or other distress.

"Yes, quite all right, thank you," he said, "just rather taken by surprise. What about your train?"

"There's one in four minutes."

"Good. Out you get then."

With evident reluctance she stepped out to the pavement, slammed the door, and stood dejectedly beside the car. It was plain that she wanted to stave off for as long as possible the dissolution of the Great Adventure. Brett realised that the end had been accelerated by his sudden withdrawal of interest, the sudden upsurge of his separate life bringing home to her the sad truth that their contact was temporary and superficial. He felt sorry for her. "Goodbye, Stephanie," he said. "Thank you for bringing back the glove."

"How do you know my name?" she asked.

"I saw it in your coat when I took it off."

"What a lot you do notice," she sighed. "Geoffrey's eyes, and this—"

For a moment Brett thought she was going to ask him his Christian name; but she didn't.

"I must go," she said abruptly. "Goodbye."

She turned and ran. Brett pushed the starter.

———

He drove home rather faster than he had driven to the station. He put the car to bed with a speed that would have lost no marks at a rally, crunched across the lawn, and thudded up the iron stairs. The flat was still in darkness; Christina had not yet come home. He let himself into the kitchen, padded through to the living room and dropped heavily into an armchair.

The situation in which he found himself could no longer be pushed to one side. He had bought for Christina a cameo brooch, the price of which had been deliberately cut. At best he could thank Majendie's desire to get him out of the shop, the blessed sanctuary. The old man, while his back was turned, must have sent Mr. Emmanuel a warning look—*this is a police inspector*; or at any rate— *this is someone I want buttered up, so give him whatever he wants at a third its price and sweep the sordid creature out of our premises.* He reflected sourly that Majendie, even in thought, would not have used the words buttered up. At worst, the Diana cameo was the beginning of blandishment, the first part of a bribe, tentative, not yet crudely offered; a persuasion not to investigate what Majendie might have to conceal, whether a link with the Karukhin affair or some other illegality.

But thirty-five pounds! he said to himself. In the context of his earned income alone, and of Majendie's lucrative trade, it seemed a ludicrous sum to take as proof of a serious intent to bribe. But, to his certain knowledge, disastrous, ramifying scandals had sprung from tinier seeds. To return the brooch and tell them what he had learnt was, however, out of the question. It was better that Majendie's, or Majendie, should believe him lulled in complaisance; at least, for a time. Besides, he didn't want to put Stephanie Cole in the black. He wondered why he should bother with her. Stephanie Cole! Yet he couldn't think of her harshly. Poor Stephanie, victim to a hazy, half-comprehended infatuation, to chafing impatience of the solid security that had coddled her; victim, perversely but inevitably, to resentment at being displaced from the position of spoilt family baby—he would have forgiven her a lot. And it would be too hypocritical in himself not to acknowledge a certain sympathy with the mainsprings, as he defined them, of her behaviour with the glove; sex, curiosity, and a desire for attention.

The telephone rang. He picked it up. "Primrose—" he began. A thick voice cut him short.

"Vat you, me ol' cock sparrer? Ow you doin'? Eh? Eh? I said, 'ow you doin', sparrer, eh?"

For a couple of seconds Brett's mind reeled, adjusting itself to work he had forgotten. Then he felt his heart give a mighty, thankful bound. "Pink! All right," he said, transferring the 'phone to his right hand and reaching for the pencil and message block.

"I bin keepin' all right too. Change me job, I 'ave. Nice little job at 'Ampstead. Eh? I said 'Ampstead. Well, ain't seen you since yer 'oliday. Ow's dear ol Ramsgit? I like it all rairn Pegwill Bay. Eh? I said Pegwill Bay. Nice. Quiet like. Useter be, anyow. Get ve jets, ese days, overin abairt. Eh? I said overin. One come dairn ve ovver week, crash like, near ve ol fort. Eh? I said near ve ol fort. ol Roman place. *You* know. Ah well, wodger doin' Chrissmas? I'm packin' up Chrissmas Eve. Eh? I said Chrissmas Eve. Ain't clockin' airt midday, rotten ol barfs. I wonarf knock off sharp six-firty. Eh? I said six-firty. Well, might be seen you sometime, sparrer, eh? Dropper ve old usual sometime, eh?"

"Certainly," said Brett. "Same place?"

"Ass me ol' sparrer! Ah well, pushin' off. Appy Chrissmass! Tooraloo!"

Brett put down the phone and studied the lines scribbled on the pad.

Hampstead Pegwell Bay hovering near the old fort Christmas Eve six thirty.

Pink. He was in the Pink. Good, useful—but not priceless—Pink. How had Pink, of all people, tuned in to the Hampstead lot? But it didn't matter, as long as this proved as sound as Pink's previous offerings. And why should it not? The old fort, the old Roman place. That would be Richborough, Rutupiae, the legions' depot. Pink was revealing unsuspected erudition. Richborough, Kent. The county would have to be asked to co-operate. And hovering—that sounded as if they would have to deal with a helicopter. He couldn't think what other meaning to put on the word. The U.S. Air Force was stationed at Manston, close by; but there would probably be some technical, legal, difficulty in getting help from them. He would have to keep it a purely police occasion; and it was obviously going to be complicated. He blenched—leave stopped over a large area, the day before Christmas!

He picked up the phone, called for a taxi in five minutes, and raced upstairs, peeling off his bright silk clothes as he ran.

Part Three

CHRISTMAS EVE

"They say no one's seen feather nor bone of Wacey," said Beddoes. "That right?"

Nightingale wearily pulled out a chair and sat down. "Beddoes, your searing zeal is ghastly. Yes. I rang when I woke. How did I manage to wake, I wonder, after about three hours' sleep." He stared out of the window of his office, at the menacing midwinter dawn. The sky bore a dirty flush, like the face of a child with measles.

"Not surprising," said Beddoes. "About Wacey, I mean," he added hastily. "By the way, after you put me down at Charing Cross yesterday I thought as I was right on top of Vanbrugh Street I'd ring up and find out which bar Wacey had been seen in, then go and look about—I know you said go home. But it was dead easy. I don't call that work. Just dropped in and started chatting in due time."

"About Wacey?"

"I may have had a tap on the loaf," said Beddoes tersely,

"but it's not hollow up there yet. I wafted out a description of Ivan the Terrible, and sure enough, they knew him. New customer, but he's shown up quite often in the past two months or so. Never any trouble, never started shouting. May have spoken to other customers on the quiet, of course—"

"But no unbosoming?"

"No. And he was last there about six o'clock on the evening of the twenty-second."

"*Our* night! He probably went along in the expectation of being met with his cut. I don't suppose they ever intended to give it to him. After all, why waste money on someone who's too dangerous to be left loose? They knew from their own, as it happened, advantageous, experience how garrulous he could become."

"So they tagged him till they could dunk him in the canal," said Beddoes thoughtfully. "Why let him go from Vanbrugh Street at all? In fact, you'd think *that* was their real reason for making the assignation, to nab him. Perhaps he took fright and shot out into the Strand before they could catch him. They must have followed him to Bright's without getting a chance in the crowds—strange luck for him. But again, why not grab him as he charged out of the house? I mean, that must have put the wind up them. An exit like a human cannon ball means something amiss. All the more reason to snaffle him before he bubbled. Remember you thought he'd run out to tell *them*? I think he was making for us. You know how Russians love to confess."

"Then why did he go to the Derby Arms? To drink himself up to it?"

"Maybe." Beddoes paused. "Poor blinking scarecrow."

Nightingale was surprised by this, from Beddoes. He

made no comment. "Have you heard about Richborough?" he asked.

"Tentatively. Who pipped?"

"Pink. That reminds me, I must remember to see that he gets his paltry due."

"Did he tell you it was the Hampstead lot?"

"Well, he made a point of the name Hampstead, and he always knows what I'm working on. Very considerate."

"Favourites. How do you do it?"

"I overlooked him once, years ago, when I was taking up a batch. I was as green as a crocus leaf. The point is, he didn't realise it was an oversight."

"And he's gone on being grateful. What time's the show?"

"Six-thirty. Kent are going into position as soon as it's dark. That means a long wait, but the thing mustn't be scotched by the untimely twinkling of a silver button. Do you know this Richborough? I've passed through, or by. It's part of the Stour estuary marsh—nothing but labyrinthine drainage ditches, river cuts, derelict wharves and sheds from the old war, and a few raw factories. They're trying to bring it to life again, I think, as some kind of port. There's a tiddy railway, power cables, and the castle, originally a Roman fort. According to Pink, that's where the helicopter's due—or nearby. So Kent will concentrate in that area." He sighed.

"Cheer up," said Beddoes. "Their coppers are better than their cricket." He smiled with as much complacency as if he personally could take credit for Surrey's place in the championship table. "What now?"

"Pink. I mustn't forget Pink. Rather sullies the purity of his gratitude, doesn't it? One day I'll introduce you by phone, then I can bequeath him to you when I go."

"Boil me! Old Pink'll be peaching on the Devil by then, won't he?"

"He's not that old. Besides—" Nightingale paused. "Suppose I were to resign?"

There was much to substantiate Beddoes' observation on Russians' love of confession. They seemed to free themselves of the burdens of conscience with greater ease and frequency than many, perhaps because the vast spaces of their country bred in them a sort of uninhibited expansiveness. Letters from Russian officials to *The Times* were usually long and diffuse; as if all Times were theirs, thought Nightingale. But while it might be possible to prove Russians statistically the greatest confessors, the urge was not peculiar to them. It was common. And Nightingale, oppressed by the matter of the cameo, which from the accretion of his knowledge and suspicions had grown to a boulder's weight, was overwhelmingly aware of it.

"Never mind," he said to the speechless Beddoes. "Majendie, now. Last night I heard, by chance, that he lives in Kent, and that there he keeps his collection. It may be coincidence, and at best it's a very tenuous link."

Beddoes looked dubious. "He's admitted an awful lot for someone in the soup. To clear his name in Olga's prayer book he need only have mentioned the brooch in the twenties, which was probably true enough."

"You surely don't imagine I told him we'd seen that address? For all he knows we may have found letters or drafts of letters—hers to him, I mean—and heaven knows what else. He *had* to cover his visit. Oh, he went, that's almost a certainty. He knew the jewels were kept in a trunk. I suppose someone could have passed that on from Ivan, but *I* didn't tell him. Anyway, he's going down to Kent today. Takes the Man of Kent to Folkestone, then drives himself."

"Folkestone's quite a way from the Stour."

"The Man of Kent arrives at Folkestone at quarter to three. The helicopter arrives at Richborough at six-thirty. Plenty of time, for all sorts of possibility."

"Such as Majendie driving a heli out of its hangar in his back garden and wafting over to Richborough. That sounds nice. Have they checked what's registered in that part?"

"He hasn't one, needless to say."

"Well, I don't get this marsh melodrama," grumbled Beddoes. "If they must be so perishing exotic as to use a heli, why not take the stuff to its base and load it there?"

"The stuff! Because the base, even if it isn't Majendie's house, will be owned by someone, and that someone could be traced, ultimately. You can't tether a helicopter in a field as if it were a goat. And that someone wouldn't want the stuff, as you elegantly put it, brought anywhere near his property. Therefore you find a place which is lonely, but reasonably *near* the base—in case unpropitious circumstances arise, and either end needs to warn off the other at the last minute— and near the coast, so that you flit off English soil as quickly as possible to your prospective market."

"Then you *do* think Majendie's house may be the base?"

"Not necessarily. Kent offers other spots."

"And what about the radar at Manston? Still, they don't chase everything that crosses it. And is Richborough on the coast?"

Brett sighed: prompted by the same heaviness as had moved him earlier, when Beddoes had mistakenly assumed him to mistrust Kent's efficiency. "The trouble is that the name Richborough is loosely applied to a large area, apart from the castle. Here, let's get the map out. In the drawer— good. You see, the castle's on the land side of those river cuts, right behind the railway, in fact. Easily accessible by road, however—I'm thinking of cars—"

"Taking the stuff to meet the heli. Well, what am I supposed to call it? Praeda?"

"On the other side of the river and the road, though, you see, Richborough is written right across the point, headland, whatever you'd call it. The land's all golf course so they'd find it difficult to take a car through in the dark. There's the coast guard rather nearer than they'd find comfortable, possibly caretakers or late workers in the factories—"

"Christmas carousal in the club house—"

"—and less features to guide them down."

"Headlights," Beddoes suggested, "*if* they could get cars through."

"That's not much. Whereas by the castle they could get their bearing from the lights of Ramsgate behind them, the road, the railway line—I know it wouldn't be lit, but they could hang right over it to make sure—and look, those big drainage cuts. Anyway, Pink specified the fort area. And the different lettering of Richborough on the point is surely to indicate the whole area once comprised the Roman port."

"Well?" said Beddoes innocently. "Who's said otherwise?"

Nightingale was silent. Beddoes must know that he had been discussing the affair with his superiors. Superior Wisdom had preferred the point as a likely landing ground, had frowned on too implicit a trust in Pink, had wanted at least to split the county's available force to watch both places. Nightingale, suffering contradiction, swallowing retorts, in the grim but ultimately successful battle to have things his own way, had passed an unpleasant half-hour, He had emerged feeling that a knot had been drawn tight inside him and that the atmospheric pressure had somehow increased.

"So we *are* watching the fort?" said Beddoes.

"Yes," said Nightingale, flushing. "You can take yourself down there in time to be in at the end."

"In what capacity?" asked Beddoes.

Nightingale had to pause again. Superior Wisdom had taken moderate umbrage at some of Beddoes' twitting which had been wafted, as Beddoes would say, to its ears. The Superior Thumb had come down unequivocally on Nightingale's proposal to give Beddoes a major part in handling the Richborough crisis; and Nightingale, conscious that insistence might lose him his whole hard-won position, had preferred to sacrifice Beddoes.

"Well, just go down," he said. "Introduce yourself to the Superintendent—he knows you're coming—"

"And take a ringside seat," concluded Beddoes. "You meanwhile—"

"I shall be following Majendie, and hoping also to roll up to Richborough in time."

Beddoes frowned. "Following? On the train and by car? Then—excuse me—but why not send me, or any old one?"

"Because if Majendie has a guilty conscience, he'll probably be sensitive to being followed, and if he looks round and sees a stranger he may take fright. Whereas I've already spent some time with him, and he's used to the idea of my interest, which must appear singularly harmless and off the track. And I think it will be all to the good, if I'm to be seen by anyone, that I should *not* be heading for Richborough this afternoon. I don't want *anyone* to take fright. I want the helicopter to go up, wherever it is."

"With any luck the light'll be too bad for *anyone* to recognise you. But why belittle your power to strike terror into Majendie?"

Nightingale shrugged. He could hardly say to Beddoes: because Majendie will think I've been softened by the preliminary *douceur*, and will only smile to see me keeping up a pretence of chasing him.

"And by the way," said Beddoes, "how do they propose to cope with a heli? Borrow one of Manston's to sit on top of it?"

"No. That was suggested—not Manston's, but another helicopter all the same. It would have meant risking entanglement and crash and fire, quite unnecessarily dangerous. Kent have something worked out, though I haven't yet had details. Perhaps you'd get them through for me—I've a few things to settle before I leave. Take a special note of the car they're to provide for me at Folkestone, and tell them I'll drive myself. Just a plain civilian car—there's no need to appropriate expensive equipment. You could ask Manston to send us a reliable weather forecast. Oh, and just see if the division has anything new. Give them another half-hour before you do that, though. All right?"

"All right," said Beddoes patiently.

Brett drove to Fitch Street. He had half intended to call again on Majendie. But on approaching the shop he was reminded by the sight of Kellett's that his brother's record token lay in his pocket. If he changed it, he would be able to play his choice at Christmas, in the unlikely event of his being free. He had time to spare. The things he had told Beddoes he had to settle could be boiled down to one thing; the cameo. He was making a little free time for himself in which he might try to work out the best solution. To buy the record would in any case take only a few minutes. Since he knew that recording and performance were excellent, he would not stop to test it; a glance at the surfaces would suffice. He parked the car, walked past Majendie's, and opened Kellett's heavy glass door.

It would have been difficult to guess, from mere appearance, what sort of shop this was, or indeed that it was a shop at all. It more resembled a superior travel agent's office, or the showroom of an air line. A sponge-backed carpet covered every inch of the floor. Behind a crescent of counter, strewn with leaflets and catalogues, half a dozen assistants were seated at regular intervals. Behind them, a wall of pressed fibrous material extended almost to the ceiling and sides of the room. Beyond this, Brett knew from past visits, another wall was formed by what looked like grooved bookcases, which held the records. Beyond that were the stairs which led up and down to displays of perfectionists' sound-reproducing equipment. Last of all lay the best insulated playing cubicles in London, the only place in the capital where Brünnhilde's Immolation could be reduced to a whisper merely by shutting a door.

Brett scanned the semicircle for the pie-eyed Geoffrey. Not finding him, he approached a rather pretty dark girl and asked for his song-cycle. She disappeared round the side of the wall to fetch it. This arrangement irritated Brett, reminding him of a women's shoe shop, where the boxes are kept out of sight and assistants trot ceaselessly to and fro in their efforts to interpret the vague demands of their customers. At least he knew exactly what he wanted.

The girl returned with his record and asked if he wished to hear it.

"No, thank you," said Brett, drawing it from its sleeve and tilting it to the light. There were no blemishes on the silky surface. He gave it back to her. "Is Geoffrey not here?" he asked.

"No," she said, surprised. Her face took on a slightly malignant expression. "He didn't have to come in today."

Geoffrey, Brett gathered, received preferential treatment

which made both him and the giver unpopular. Brett thought he probably deserved to be. From what Stephanie reported of his instructive conversation, he sounded as repulsive a puppy as he looked. Brett suspected that the design behind his musical evangelism was so to impress Stephanie that he could, at a well-judged moment, trade on her wish not to be thought lacking in the sophistication, as she might imagine it, compatible with such cleverness.

Brett caught himself up; he was judging Geoffrey rashly. At least Geoffrey hadn't smirked at Majendie's invitation to see his collection, which was more than he could claim for himself.

He received his record, wrapped, and as he did so a swiftly smothered susurrus of excitement passed round the semi-circle. Knowing that he was not the cause, he turned to look through the window to the street.

Outside Kellett's a Solomon's temple of a car had drawn to the kerb. A chauffeur stepped out to open the door, and a tall fat man emerged. He wore soft, mushroom-coloured clothes, a large hat reminiscent of a sombrero, and dark glasses. Brett recognised him at once; Anatole Guzmann, a cosmopolitan of bewilderingly mixed origin and stupefying wealth. He was addicted to the collection of recorded music, his list of which was reputed to be fantastically long, interesting and valuable; and his pursuit of phonographic rarities had reached the proportion of mania. This much was common knowledge; or, if not common, it could be acquired from anyone conversant with the gramophone world. What was not generally known was that Anatole Guzmann, about a year before, had figured on the fringes of a notorious European scandal, from which he was extricated only by the influence his money could command. For Brett, Guzmann would never free himself from the unsavoury miasma which seeped from the affair; but he doubted whether Kellett's, even if they knew of it, would consider Guzmann's money contaminated.

As he doubted, one of the assistants, obsequiousness ironed out of his face, was opening the door for Guzmann; who, secure in the knowledge that he was the most valued item at present in the shop, moved across the floor with the unhurried purposefulness of a pregnant woman, with the same certainty that no one would importunately jostle the burden he carried in front of him. About eight months, thought Brett unkindly, eyeing Guzmann from the side as he went round the fibre screen. He would be going to the office of Mr. Kellett, if such a person existed. Would he, the manager, the director, come scuttling down in person to the shelves to find Mr. Guzmann's choice? That choice would be, doubtless, too valuable to be kept in the main shop, even though the vulgar herd was never allowed to browse there.

"I think," said Brett, on an inexplicable impulse, "I'll look over the recorders while I'm here. They're still displayed upstairs?"

"Yes, sir," said the girl, bored, "round the screen and take the stairs to your left."

Brett obeyed, acknowledging to himself that he was slightly mad. He passed the record shelves, and paused for a minute at the foot of the stairs. On his right was the cash desk, which was so situated that anyone leaving the playing cubicles could not avoid passing it. If they wanted to buy the record they had finished hearing, they handed it to the cashier, who placed it on a latex-padded conveyor belt which ran from her desk to the front of the shop, where the record was wrapped while the customer paid.

He ran up the stairs, which took a turn to the right and led to the display of equipment, arranged on a handsome dark orange carpet and white tables. He glanced round quickly. As he had expected, Anatole Guzmann was not to be seen. At the back of the room, separated by a wood and glass partition, was an apartment which was devoted to the needs of those who possessed and wished to play vintage and veteran records. It was just possible that Guzmann might be in there. Brett crossed the room and looked through the glass. The apartment was empty.

He turned back towards the head of the stairs. Immediately to the left of them as one came up was a swing door, marked private, giving on a corridor. Brett guessed that the rooms adjoining this corridor were offices, not, perhaps managerial offices. But as the basement held only wirelesses, he was sure that Guzmann would be in this part of the building; and he was determined to find out.

An assistant was approaching. "Can I help you, sir?" he asked; or rather, suggested. Brett neither paused nor deflected his course. "No, thank you," he said coldly. That answer, in that voice, had never yet failed him; it didn't now. The assistant stopped in his tracks, and Brett pushed open the door.

As it swung to, he realised that the corridor was a cul de sac. He must either return foolishly in front of the assistant, so foolishly as to appear suspicious, or plunge into one of the offices and concoct a fable to account for his presence. The latter would be embarrassing especially if he burst in on Guzmann and whoever had invited him—the hypothetical Mr. Kellett. Altogether he was walking as slowly as he dared, the need to make up his mind was pressing. He had already passed one door. He would, he decided, go to the window which ended the corridor, look through for a minute, then return to the shop and get out at full speed. If challenged by an assistant, he would imply that he was a surveyor. If someone came out of the offices, he would trust to his powers of extempore invention. But suddenly he saw that they would not be tested. The door frame at the far end of the right wall held no door; it opened not on a room but on a downward flight of steps. Plainly a conversion had at some time been made in the building.

He was relieved; but in case the assistant should be watching him through the glass of the swing doors he paused for a moment at the window before turning down the stairs, in order to avoid giving an impression of nervous haste. He found himself looking down on the 'back alley', as Stephanie called it. And as he stood there, a sound began faintly. It came, he judged from the room on the right, which had been truncated to make way for the stairs. Someone in there was playing a record of *O Paradiso*.

Brett moved down to the second stair, temporarily hidden from anyone. The record was an old one. Even allowing for the muffling effect of a wall, he could detect the flat background, so different from the vaulted resonance beloved of modern electrical engineers. He was puzzled that he was able to hear it at all. The new wall was, no doubt, for structural reasons, comparatively thin. He studied it; and saw, near the top and near where he stood, a ventilating grille, through which the sound issued.

He held his breath and strained his ears, just discerning a piano accompaniment, a tinny oscillation well at the back of the vocal line. As usual, the voice had suffered less from the deficiencies of the infant science. It did not sound as if it were being squeezed out of the skylight of some physical attic, as is often the way with tenors. It was open, virile, even in tone, effortlessly smooth, and of an unforced power which indicated reserves on which the singer had never needed to draw. Yet strength was combined with taste and expressiveness. This man, thought Brett, was a tenor and a half.

He had made no study of the Golden Age. Such records as he knew had been heard by chance, with the exception of an ancient *Rigoletto* quartet which Christina had picked up for a couple of marks and accordingly treasured, but which he privately thought sounded like four mice and a guitar. The names of a few tenors were familiar, but not their styles or voices. He felt that he would recognise Caruso, and that this singer was not Caruso, nor, probably, Italian. The vocal timbre had something of the sweetness which is characteristic of certain Slavs; and Brett received the impression, although he could not be sure because of the wall, that the aria was sung, after all, in French. Jean de Reszke, he thought, with irony; and then, with a sensation of having turned a double somersault, *Jean de Reszke.*

Guzmann and his passion for Golden Age plums. Kellett's, next door to Majendie's. Prince Sevastyan Karukhin, who had a flat in Paris, who was anxious to rival the collection of Count Vyestnitsky—

Brett was fortunately not so carried away that he lost his senses. He became conscious that an alien sound was imposed on the aria; the jerky pounding of a pair of heavy female feet clad in high-heeled shoes; feet which were coming down the corridor towards him.

He couldn't wait to hear the putative Jean so much as finish his phrase. His toes barely touched the edges of the stair treads as he ran down, ankles yielding springily from long practice in his own home. The stairs debouched down the side of a small room with two cubicles at one end, wash basins, a mirror, and a row of pegs hung with women's coats.

He realised in a kind of calm alarm that it must be the women staff's cloakroom. He had no time to hesitate about going through the only door. To meet someone on its threshold or to be found inside by the high-heeled woman would be equally embarrassing. The heels were shaking the top stairs. He went out.

He found himself in a narrow passage at the back of what he recognised as playing cubicles. If, when he came to the end of them, he turned left, he would eventually arrive at the desk, the conveyor belt, the front of the shop and freedom. But if any of the assistants upstairs had watched him along the corridor and had seen him disappear down those stairs, they might have spread the word that a man was loitering in the women's lavatories. It would be unseemly if he were detained on such a suspicion as he made his way out. He chose the alternative course of keeping straight on. There was a door ahead; its position so corresponded with that of the one he'd just left that he guessed it must open on the men's cloakroom. As the wall on his right was the outer rear wall of the building, he thought it likely that he would also find an exit to Stephanie's back alley, although it was hard to see why such an exit should be denied to the women staff.

He slipped past the end of the passage which flanked the cubicles. His ear caught a snatch of whooping Strauss horns, muted to elfland dimensions. He pulled swiftly at the door, and entered. He was in the men's cloakroom, and it was empty. This room, unlike the women's had a second door, which he approached with considerably less brio. He judged that he was by now in that part of the building which lay at right angles to the main shop and met the similar projection of Majendie's across the back of the bomb site.

Brett quietly opened the door, and was confronted by a

flap of grubby green felt, hanging from top to bottom of the frame. It was the sort of thing to rouse dormant childhood terrors, despite its obvious acoustic purpose. Very cautiously he peeped round the edge of the curtain. It concealed nothing more frightening than a wide garage, rather untidily kept, clearly never free from the aftermath of unpacking. The doors were rolled completely back, revealing the cobbled alley, and letting the miserable dun daylight seep in. Two vans stood side by side in the garage. The grey and yellow stripes of the one further from Brett were familiar, Kellett's own mark. The other was smaller, quite plain, and as far as could be distinguished in the dull light, dark blue in colour. Between this van and the felt curtain two men, with their backs to Brett, were sitting on upturned boxes. They were doing nothing; not smoking, naturally enough, in a garage; but not drinking tea, not even talking, just sitting. Brett, who neither revelled in statistics of workers' idleness nor took it for granted, was surprised. Such utter immobility and lack of communication was out of place. So was something else. Neither of the men was dressed suitably for greasy work among cars and crates; one wore a blue suit the other a jacket and flannels. Suddenly, the definition of their attitude came to him. They were waiting.

He studied the two backs carefully; neither was familiar to him. But that wasn't to say he would be as much a stranger to the men. He decided to withdraw through the shop after all; and was just gently letting back the felt curtain when his eye fell on something that made him pause.

A block of three stone steps led down from his feet to the floor of the garage. In the corner formed by their projection from the wall, on the side further from the alley, was stacked a pair of number plates.

Brett couldn't see more than the end figure. For a second

or two he wondered if he might succeed in picking them up quite noiselessly and making off. He decided that he ought not to try, closed the felt and, silently, the door. He let himself calmly out of the lavatory, strode down the passage between the cubicles, and raised his wrapped record to the cashier, hoping her to be unobservant in nature or mood, and therefore not to have noticed so much as that a particular customer had earlier gone up the stairs, still less that he now reappeared on the ground floor without having come down them. He was in the front of the shop. No one challenged him; no one looked at him. He was out.

He stood for a moment staring idly at Guzmann's car. He's a nine thousand pounder, or I am a bounder, he thought, adapting the poet. He needed now to see whether *Majendie's* garage offered anything of interest; but he didn't want to show himself, or, indeed, any detective, in the back alley. He glanced at his watch, and along the street towards Majendie's.

Two boys walked past him. Automatically he assigned them to the fifth form. Their school caps were navy blue, with two white bands, and the badge, which Brett had not seen for some years, was a castle gate. He stared after the boys at first rather ruefully, then thoughtfully; then he fell in behind them.

He allowed them to walk a good way along the street, so that they were well out of sight of Kellett's, before he overtook them. They were engaged in an animated and unseasonal discussion of cricket.

"Good morning," he said.

To his pleasure, they returned the greeting with faultless alacrity. He introduced himself. The inevitable reaction of alarm was succeeded by a sharp interest, quickly subdued to polite proportions. One of the pair, indeed, seemed to be suffering a certain doubt.

"I'm afraid I can't give you more than a private visiting card," said Brett, producing it and handing it to the doubter. "But you can ring—you know the number—to establish that I am who I claim to be. Only would you do that, please, *after* you've done something for me?"

The doubter looked from the card in his hand to Brett.

"May I keep this, sir?" he asked.

"Please do," Brett enjoyed a moment's prevision of the card liberally dusted with finger-print powder.

"Thank you, sir." The doubter, apparently fortified, put the card carefully in a rather new wallet. "What are we to do?"

"You see the gap between the milliner's and the art dealer's a little along the pavement? That leads through to an alley running parallel with the street. I want you to walk back along that alley, talking just as you were, looking, perhaps, as if you were dead keen to explore London's byways or some such thing. When you've gone about forty yards you'll see a garage, doors open, in which are two vans, one grey and yellow, the other dark blue or green. Memorise the number of the dark one if you can, and if it's visible. Then look at the very next garage. If it's closed, well, that can't be helped. If it's open, see what vehicles, if any, are inside, and whether any men. If it's empty, take as thorough a general impression as you can *while you're walking by.* All this must be done absolutely casually. No one will be on the look-out, no one will think anything of seeing you, but obviously you don't want to peer. You'll come to a second gap leading to the street. Go through, and meet me at the telephone box at the corner of Fitch Street and the Square. You've absolutely nothing to worry about. All right?"

"Yes, sir. Starting now?"

"Starting now."

Brett turned round, crossed the road, and walked back

on the other side of Fitch Street. Guzmann's car was still outside Kellett's. He reached the corner and went into the telephone box.

He found the number of a certain phonographic eminence, and dialled. The eminence, by good fortune, was at home. Brett, unwilling to cause alarm, presented himself not in his official capacity, but as a gramophone enthusiast connected with the North-West London Opera Group, two of whose productions the eminence had attended and had been heard to commend. The eminence was gracious. He assured Brett that, apart from some exceedingly rare and unsatisfactory cylinders taken from the flies of the Metropolitan during a performance of *L'Africaine*, in which the singer was almost drowned by extraneous noise, no records of the voice of Jean de Reszke were known certainly to exist. He confirmed that a privately made disc would command a fabulous price from a person sufficiently interested and wealthy. Brett mentioned Anatole Guzmann. The eminence regretted, with marked distance, that he was unacquainted with either Mr. Guzmann's list or his personal predilections. Brett thanked him, and rang off.

He looked out of the cell-like windows. The two boys were coming across the road at what could be called a brisk saunter. If they'd carried that off all along the alley Brett thought, they were a credit to the school.

"Any luck?" he asked, pushing open the door as they appeared beside it.

"Yes, sir," said the erstwhile doubter, all eagerness.

"There weren't any men, but there was an estate car, a blue Morris Oxford, quite new."

"Did you get its number—and the other?"

The second boy, who had not spoken since saying good morning, handed Brett a piece of paper.

"Good Lord! You didn't stand outside and take notes?"

"No, sir, in the passage," said the doubter, with a look of indignant reproach.

"And that's all?"

"There wasn't much else to notice. It was just a garage."

"Tidier than the other," put in the quiet boy.

"All right," said Brett, "that's fine. What are your names?"

The doubter hesitated. "Will what we did ever be made public?" he asked.

"Not if you don't wish it," said Brett, "but I'd like to tell the head. One thing—I hardly *need* ask, I know, but I must—don't speak about this, even to your families, until I let you know that you may. I will, I promise. At least you can discuss it between yourselves, so you won't quite burst! May I have those names?"

They gave him their names, said goodbye, and walked away. Brett put his hand to the door of the telephone box.

"Sir!"

He turned. The doubter had run back.

"Sir, we didn't tell you our addresses."

"I'll do it through the school."

"Do you know the school, sir?"

"I was there myself. All right?"

The doubter nodded. "Oh yes. Quite all right."

Brett made a call to the office, to the effect that someone should be sent to keep an eye on the two exits from the back alley, with instructions to report the appearance of either or both of the vans he described. He gave the numbers, with a qualification that they should not be relied on. Then he walked along to his car.

He noticed suddenly how dark the sky had grown. It was a dirty yellowish grey, like an old ill-laundered pillow case swollen to bursting with feathers. He flicked on his sidelights. Soon there would be snow.

Would Majendie, unless innocent, have gone to the absurd length of mentioning the Princess's record? He must have thought it wise to cover everything he'd seen. And he *had* intended to give them—to *give* them!—to Kellett's. That was an admission which sailed near the wind. Brett remembered, as if it were an age past, a moment in which Kellett's had seemed merely grubby, not over anxious to know whether the record had been honestly come by, knowing only that they could sell if for whatever they asked—of the right person. He had thought Guzmann was their choice because other collectors of as great reputation but of better repute would have wanted assurances, proof, of the record's provenance. But he had come to believe that Kellett's were in no doubt at all of that. Majendie and Kellett's, or someone in Kellett's, worked together; and Geoffrey worked for them. The musical know-all cultivated Stephanie not with a view to a seduction, thought that might go with the job, but to discover whether from the bomb site one could hear sounds from the adjacent cellars, whether she had ever so heard anything; further, to elicit from her artless conversation whether anything could be or ever had been observed at Majendie's which might give rise to suspicion. Geoffrey didn't have to come in this morning—because he was busy elsewhere? Majendie, stressing his dislike of Kellett's, pulling a face, so unnecessarily, at their very name, fuming when they complained—warned?—about Stephanie. Had he fumed for her sake? No, but because they had sent the message in so rudely; that was to say, with such deplorable lack of prudence, publicising their interest in the bomb site. And why did Kellett's, with their roomy shop, want the bomb site?

So that they themselves, rather than some curious outsider, should cover their cellars.

He must have to deal, he realised, with the person who was the mainspring of Kellett's. No subordinate could have got away with it. With what? With using the cellars to store stolen Nymphenburg figures and Fabergé cigarette cases? Those efficient robberies, that efficient shop! The conclusion that they matched, that they were products of the same organising brain, was at once wild and feasible. But how Superior Wisdom would have received a request for a squad to raid the cellars of Kellett's and Majendie's Brett shuddered to imagine. Perhaps it was as well that the moment for such action had passed. For the cellars, so near the time of the helicopter's arrival, would be innocent enough, unless indeed there was something left for another occasion.

The van and the estate car were the things to keep in sight. He felt, very strongly, that they were waiting to set out for Richborough. Feeling was not the safest basis of action. But to write off the chance as too far-fetched to take was something he might afterwards regret. Six-thirty. Unless they were to make wide precautionary detours, or were to call somewhere else in their way, the vans need not set out so very soon. Yet the men had seemed ready, just waiting the word to go. He frowned. Even if they were to start now, they were almost bound to take the A2 out of London; and in any case, with someone covering the alley exits—they should be already in position—the numbers would be passed to the patrols. With the further assistance of Christmas traffic congestion, they should be picked up easily enough. And in the light of new circumstances, Beddoes should and would be one of those who did the picking.

———

"Just what I like," said Beddoes, "minicars with Rolls-Royce engines. Three! Boil me! Not sparing the lolly, are we. Why not ask for reliefs at Rochester, say, and Sittingbourne?"

Brett, whose application for the cars had already drawn from above some aphorisms on extravagance, scalded Beddoes with a look he had bottled up before others. "Because the vans may turn off A2. The more I think of it, the more likely it seems that they'll take a meandering, misleading course. I don't know why they've not started already. You can take over from each other as you please—fix a timetable before you start, or use the wireless, whichever you like." He secretly hoped they would use the wireless; having been reproached in advance with extravagance, he would be sorry not to fulfil expectation. "Don't you think," he said, "it would be absurdly clumsy to trail behind them with the same car from London to Canterbury? If you did that you'd be lucky to get as far as Chatham. Then they'd try twisting about, or brazenly stop and make a phone call, thumbing their noses at you the while, or start speeding in a panic and crash into a wall. So by a message or by default of a message or by failure to pass a checkpoint, they'd give warning to the others to melt away from Richborough. They mustn't be stopped, they mustn't be frightened." He paused. "What about the weather?"

"Two falls already at Manston," said Beddoes, gloomily, "and their weather cocks say there's a real bliz blowing in. Poor old Kent, sitting in a snow pack. What was that happened to Lord Bacon's chicken?"

"It happened to him, not the chicken, and he wasn't Lord Bacon, he was Lord Verulam. Anything from the division?"

"They found Ivan's doctor. Turned all starch and profes-sional confidence. Not a pip. Pity he has his surg in a rented room. Divi slipped round the back and had a word with Mrs. Flannery, who, needless to say, has her eyeful of all the patients. Since the N.H.S. started Ivan's propped up the wall once a week without fail. Drops for his nose and flannels for his chest and a few gallons a year of coloured water. About a month ago he complained to the assembled sick of Islington that he was sleeping badly."

"Did they find out whether he has a regular dispenser?"

"No. They've started to look."

"It doesn't matter. Quite obvious, isn't it?"

"Yes—phenobarb, one a night for a month, probably fifty at a time. Quite enough. By the way, Ivan also sounded the doctor, or said he was going to, on the possibility of having Gran certified."

"When?"

"Months and months ago. Nothing came of it, appar-ently. I suppose you can't shove people in already bursting institutions unless they're raising Cain. One thing more. There's a family called Endean living at number six. The daughter dropped in at the station this morning on her way to work—she'd been out when the divi called in my unfortunate absence—and she said she'd met the old woman from num-ber thirteen on the evening of Saturday a fortnight past—and I wouldn't have bothered you with it only I thought at the time it was odd and now in the circumstances—et cetera."

"You don't mean she met her in the street?"

"Yes. The girl was on her way to a dance, which is how she can be sure it was Saturday. As she turned the corner from Bright's into the High Street she all but knocked Olga down. She was coming into the Row."

"Ivan would be at the Oak Tree, I suppose. What about Mrs. Minelli? She didn't mention that Mrs. Karukhin had ever been out."

"Boil me! She wasn't sitter-in to Olga. I expect she was out herself."

"Yes, yes. Saturday evening—going to confession, perhaps."

"And Olga?" asked Beddoes innocently.

"Coming back from the pillar box to which she'd consigned a letter to Majendie, as if you hadn't worked that out for yourself."

"But you're still going after the old bird?"

"Why not?"

Beddoes picked up a paper clip and began to make a great labour of straightening it. "All right. It's up to you, of course."

"Thank you. There's something I haven't told you, but I can't wait now to restate the case—*ab ovo*. What car for me at Folkestone?"

"A silver-grey '55 Wyvern. Here's the number." Beddoes handed Brett, with such a show of long-suffering as he could not miss, a slip of paper. "The boot's open and the key's under the bit of rag at the back." He paused. "Suppose Majendie teams up with a whole fleet?"

"I should hope to recognise some of his associates."

"So long as you don't try to tackle a crowd singlehanded, or something daft. I mean," Beddoes went on very quickly, reddening, as if even he felt this remark to be somewhat outspoken, "they've got Olga to account for this time, not just a lot of china. Start poking them about and anyone'd have one foot in the grave—and the other on a banana skin."

"Such solicitude!"

Beddoes into two seconds compressed a mime of nauseated repudiation, then switched his face back to normal.

"And suppose the old bird's all right?" he asked, springing the question with all its load of doubt as if he hoped to knock Brett off balance.

"Then I shall be more relieved than you can know or imagine," replied Brett quietly. "And now we'd better set out. Everything seems ready."

"Meeting at Canterbury after the show, I suppose?" said Beddoes in a rather chastened voice. "I say—suppose Majendie sees you at Charing Cross?"

"You think no one but you knows how to board a train decently? And I'm travelling in the van."

"No nice B.R. lunch?"

"I'm having that before I start."

Beddoes glanced at the clock. "Time for soup and a spud, anyway. Considerate of those vans to hang about like this, isn't it? You should see what the canteen's packed for us. Flasks of soup, cold turkey, rolls, mince pies, coffee—"

"Kippers and custard."

"All right, I'm going. I say—" Beddoes' face brightened irrepressibly. "Remember that time Old Thing tipped the wrong thermos into his cup and poured oxtail soup on top of his milk and sugar?"

———

The Man of Kent was running into Folkestone forty minutes late. That wasn't bad, Brett thought, considering they'd had to struggle through the fall-out of a celestial pillow fight, Beddoes' bliz, which had blown in across the Channel. But the journey had seemed doubly tedious to him, cooped in the guard's van. How did they advertise for guards, he wondered—*agoraphobes only need apply?* He stretched himself, and peered through his prison window. Since Ashford there had been a respite, an insecure lull under a dark sky which threatened the approach of more than dusk. The landscape was transfigured. Its luminous desolation seemed insubstantial, almost lunar; only the hills were the wrong shape. The blanched humps of the North Downs were ribbed with shadowy patches, the caprices of wind and drifting, or underlying earthworks, Roman or British. The hills reminded Brett of the malevolent whale, with his wrinkles and scars and tangled irons. And for all their ghostly air he would find them as forbidding, as indomitable, when he was creeping up their slippery sides in a strange car to which, he was sure, no one would have had opportunity or forethought to fit chains.

The train was slackening speed. Effort was no longer to be felt, only momentum; a powerful glide, nicely controlled, smoothly braked. The guard slid back his door, and a crust of snow plopped off the roof like sugar icing from a cut cake. The wind was the knife, thought Brett, a veritable cutlass slicing great swathes out of him. He leaned out behind the guard and watched a toy station coming to meet them. There was one long narrow platform at their side, with an exit too near the back of the train for his liking, offering little cover. He was puzzled. Why such a tiny doll's house of a place? But this was the town, not the boat station: nor a terminus like Brighton, but a stop in a lateral line; clean and countrified, gamboge and green, like every Southern station, perhaps to suggest the accessibility of sand and sea, but, in midwinter, infinitely bleak.

The train stopped. He stood back, watching the doors spread open like scarab wings. And first out was Stephanie, golden head bare, wearing her yellow raincoat and a slung bag. Clearly, she knew this journey well, and had the train taped. Three steps took her from door to barrier. Her feet were nimble, but thinly shod for snow. Swift as a bird, a golden oriole, she was through the gate and gone. But where, Brett wondered, was her butter-tongued rotundity of an employer? He'd made for the dining car at Charing Cross. Was he still there, snoozing past his stop to Dover?

He appeared at that moment, clutching the little dressing case Brett had marked earlier. He was with an elderly woman; probably no more than a friend met on the train. Brett hesitated. Should he scoot out before him? He decided he hadn't time. Majendie was too near the barrier. He'd be seen. He could afford to wait for a minute, as the train wasn't yet leaving. But he wished Majendie wouldn't stroll so leisurely towards the gate, blethering the while to his friend. Five yards, three, two, Brett counted; there.

With a hasty goodbye to the guard Brett stepped down and walked along the platform, discreetly close to the office doors. He had to give the old fellow time, to allow for the prolixity of his farewells. He reached the collector and sheltered behind him, looking through the barrier. He saw Majendie's back, and the woman's, and a well-oiled stream of taxis, their fares whisked off as swiftly as records on Kellett's conveyor belt. There were handshakes now. The friend was going. And what was this? A taxi, Majendie was taking a taxi. Brett, confounded, caught its number as it swung away. He slipped his ticket to the collector and darted out.

His eyes, searching for a silver-grey Wyvern, registered a long downward slope on the right, more swooping taxis, a wall parallel with the station fence. The number suddenly leapt at him. He ran unsteadily to the snow-caked boot, wrenched it open, flicked back the rag and grabbed the key. Majendie's taxi was at the bottom, turning right. Right? Into the town. Then he'd catch him, if the engine held a spark of life.

He slammed the door, switched on, and pushed the starter. The engine sang out. With an exultant thrust of the foot he launched the car down the gravel-strewn slope. At the bottom he slowed, nosed out to the road, which was clear, and swung right. The wheels slithered ominously; but in a second the warning flew from his head. Majendie's taxi had stopped at the kerb, and Majendie himself was getting out. Brett passed quickly, and about thirty yards ahead pulled in and twisted in his seat. Majendie had crossed the road to a bus stop. Someone moved forward, someone dressed in yellow. Stephanie. Majendie was talking to her. There was a momentary hesitation; then both of them were coming back to the taxi. Thoughtfully, Brett turned to his wheel. It seemed that Majendie had offered her a lift—all the way home? That would be generous of him; and somewhat inconsistent with his predictable activities, if he were all that Brett suspected. But they were coming. Brett retrieved an imaginary object from the floor, although he doubted whether they could have identified a baboon at the wheel in the rapidly worsening visibility. He switched on sidelights, and set himself to cling inconspicuously to their tail.

But if the taxi driver was willing to take Majendie over the Downs, the roads up there couldn't be too bad; so why didn't Majendie want to drive himself, as he usually did? Or did he? Stephanie had said he kept his car at Folkestone station. But where were the garages, the lockups? There had been not so much as a padlock, an oily rag, to be seen. Because she was connected with Majendie must he distrust even her, despite her youth, her broadcasting of Majendie's residence and other leading lines, and the entire impact of her personality? In a professional manner he hardened his heart, and prepared to accept the worst; finding the process unexpectedly painful.

He followed a turn to the left, between trim villas and deserted gardens, and was fortunately alert enough to pull behind a parked van as the taxi stopped some way ahead. Startled and curious, he peeped out to look at them. Majendie was paying off the taxi; and as it moved away, he opened the side gate of one of the neat houses and walked up the path to its garage. He was going to unlock it.

Brett wondered why the old man couldn't have found something closer to the station. But that mattered less than that Stephanie was partially vindicated. Had she said Folkestone station, or just Folkestone? He couldn't remember. Quickly he took out his map and folded it so that the Folkestone to Canterbury area would remain face upmost. Barton, Majendie's village, lay about a mile from A2. It was a strange country for him to inhabit. Kent, sir—everybody knows Kent—apples, cherries, hops, and women. And blizzards, added Brett. He found Pettinge, some three miles to the east of Majendie's road. Was he going to take her? Would he, if he had other interests to watch this afternoon—unless she shared those interests? Brett tried again to think dispassionately along this line. He soon gave up. He did not want to accept it before facts forced him to. He would sooner discover Majendie to be as pure as the drift on a neighbouring privet hedge, and himself to be deluded, a fool on a wild goose chase, than believe Stephanie an accomplice.

But they were coming out of the garage. Brett, flinging the map on the seat beside him, exclaimed softly. Majendie, dear old-fashioned fellow to the last, was perched at the wheel of an enormous black box, thirty years old if it were a day, and wanting only oak and brass and lilies to make it the complete hearse. Brett was quite sure, however, that the engine wouldn't grumble at the hills. He gave them a fair start, then followed.

Majendie, he thought. Majendie? The doubt and uncertainty which had wreathed him from his first appearance had by no means finally cleared in Brett's mind. There were the letters from Olga, for instance. He didn't need to wait for a report to tell him that they were genuine. Majendie couldn't have fabricated them overnight. He *might* have had them stored against such a contingency. Brett shook his head. What was he to make of Olga's unprecedented Saturday night excursion, if not that she was slinking out to post them—omitting the formality of a stamp. It was, in fact, only too easy to see Majendie as the victim of circumstances. The dressing case? No more than that. *Common Law and the Common Man*? A legal complication arising from the course of normal business. Even Kellett's. That record—de Reszke, indeed! How much more likely to have been some other ancient tenor. Geoffrey's advances to Stephanie could bear the simplest, and his original, interpretation. There could be an excuse for those number plates. If the vans had really been waiting, if he had not in his suspicious way read too much into too little, why should it follow that Richborough was their destination? Suppose, he thought, they never started. Beddoes might be sitting at this moment, vainly repining for liberty. Brett could well imagine the assumed spaniel eyes of reproach in store, if that should prove the case; not that spaniels had such cerulean eyes. On the other hand the disappointment might be so sharp as to pierce, for once, that triple bronze of slang and twang and flippancy, and present him, for no effort, the cunningly sought and long despaired of prize, a piece of Beddoes' mind.

The road out of Folkestone climbed; a long slithering

climb. He had to stare hard to keep sight of the old black fly crawling ahead. Did every criminal drive such a deadly respectable vehicle? Why not, he asked himself, overtake, leave him standing, give him up, make for Richborough? But there was still the cameo, the tainted present, the affronting bribe, its very paltriness aggravating the offence, with all its contemptuous assessment of his price. Majendie, somehow, somewhere *had* offended in a double sense; and Brett was clinging to him for a double satisfaction.

A few flakes of snow scudded horizontally across the screen. Behind him he could see one car, catching up; and a plum-red bus, white-whiskered like Father Christmas trundled timidly downhill. Brett drove round a bend, and at once saw why the bus had hugged the far verge. On the left, the land dropped as if it had been scooped away by a gigantic soup ladle. The road crept round the hillside by courtesy of the Ancients, who had cut a ledge there with their earthworks. For good measure the bend was double; and the lightly packed snow carpet was not helpful.

At this place, the car following elected to pass. Brett's casual glance in the mirror sharpened quickly as he saw the radiator nudging out behind him. He must either shoot forward on the slippery curve, blocking the road, or draw closer to the edge to give the other room. He did neither. He simply held on, trying not to think of what would happen if another bus swung round the approaching bend. The car passed close, uncomfortably close, cleared, swerved back in front of him and raced recklessly on. Uncouth maniac, Brett commented to himself. Christmas. The party spirit. One for the road. Swilled insolence. He half hoped the homicidal lout would skid and bucket over the side; but the lights remained on the road, which now ran straight. At least that meant Majendie couldn't be crowded in such a nasty spot, not that *he* mattered, but he had a passenger; for the funereal antiquity had reached the end of the drop. Or so he thought. Thickening snow and darkness made it increasingly hard to see Majendie's lights.

The road, here ceased to rise, crossed a gently undulating plateau. Scanty habitation of shacks and bungalows clung to its lifeline. The gradients were easy, but the snow had piled deeper, and was now cascading down. In spite of this, Brett put on a spurt lest he should miss Majendie's turn to Pettinge. He sighed. Why wind down country lanes after Majendie? Why not keep on the main road to Barton, Majendie's own village, and watch him arrive? But then, after all, Majendie might not.

All at once he found himself isolated. A whirling, fragmented blanket of snow had swallowed the lights, the road, everything. He crawled on. If this choked him, so it must Majendie, who must also dawdle and struggle, and feel a similar disquiet at the clogging round the wheels. Could even a helicopter battle through such a storm, Brett wondered. The snow lifted freakishly, revealing a long avenue of clarity. He saw bosky country on either hand; and far in front, dim red pinpricks. That was either Majendie or the hog who had passed on the bend. How had they drawn so far ahead? Majendie had hurried, whether they were his lights or the other's. Why? Because he had seen at Folkestone who was following him in the grey Wyvern?

The snow came down again in a great white blot, Beddoes' bliz, full scale and strength. Brett, watching his windscreen wipers slide jerkily to and fro, wondered how soon they would stop their squeaky protests and go on strike. Woods flanked the road, as he'd been able to see in that clear half minute, so the branch to Pettinge must be near. He could no more hope to see the far side than the moon. He ground on, in a gear which depressed him. But it was his low crawl which saved him from missing the almost obliterated sign: Pettinge 2.

To prospect for traffic was pointless. The snow was a ready-made shroud, and only speed could serve him. In one sweep he cut right across the road. The wheels slipped, and he couldn't find the verge. Then he saw that he'd pulled into the mouth of the lane itself, straightened too quickly, and felt another skid. He didn't like it above half, but he was committed; the land was too narrow to turn in. He went on, and down, through snow which flew so stiflingly against the windows that he wanted all the time to be coughing. The engine was sighing in a plaintive fashion. He glanced at his speed. Ten! Even that was reckless. The road dipped, and turned. Or did it? He realised that he was encased. The window cleaners had stopped, stuck, struck; and the screen had crusted in a couple of seconds. He opened the window, leaned out, and quickly withdrew. All that had gained him was blindness, suffocation and a soaked collar. There was nothing to be done but stop, get out, and try to set the flippers to rights.

He pulled in to the left; and the car lurched and sank. He heard himself utter the most odd muted squawk as he smacked on the brake, then the handbrake. Bog, quicksand, jelly, flashed through his mind before the obvious word came. A drift. He had tipped into a drift.

He put the car quickly into reverse, eased out the handbrake, and ground his right foot to the floor. The engine uttered a petulant whine. The wheels were spinning to no effect. He tried again, with the result, it seemed to him, that the car settled at a slightly steeper angle. He stopped and sat still for some seconds, venting his feelings in his very worst curses, vehement and monosyllabic. Then he scrambled over the back of the seat. He pulled his scarf from round his neck, twisted it into some sort of protection for his head and ears, and turned up the collar of his coat. Opening the rear door, he stretched out a leg to test the depth of the snow. At this point it lay only about four inches deep. With a groan and a final imprecation he got out of the car, shut the door, and groped towards the radiator.

The car was tilted forward and to the left. After two steps, his feet plunged suddenly into deeper snow and started to slip. He caught at the angle of windscreen and bonnet, pulled himself up, turned his back to the driving snow so that he might breathe more easily, and wiped the cold encrustation from his eyelashes. He gathered that in pulling blindly to the left he had driven into a ditch which was in any case concealed by the snow that filled it. Since he had sunk at low speed into a sort of cushion, he doubted whether the car had received more than superficial damage, even if so much. But the very downy stuff which had acted as shock absorber made it impossible to pull out, and at every moment was piling deeper. What was worse, the snow and the darkness made hopeless a search for wood, old bramble, anything that might be flung down to give purchase to the back wheels.

The road was lonely, unclassified. The chance of someone coming now, in either direction, was remote; their ability, in the event, to help him, not worth counting on. If he sat in the car he would soon be snowed under. There was only one thing to be done. He must walk back to A260 in the hope that traffic would still be passing along it and that someone would give him a lift.

He brought his wrist close to his eyes and looked at the pale marks of his watch. Quarter past four. He opened the rear door, leaned across the seat to get the map, and shone his torch on it. His heart sank. Even if he were lucky enough to pick up a lift as soon as he reached the main road and were driven quickly to Canterbury—which meant, in such weather, at an average twenty—could he hope to be at Richborough in time? Six-thirty sharp, Pink had said. He doubted if he could do it.

He sat down on the edge of the seat, the map dangling from his hand and felt himself dredged by disappointment and despair. Deprived of a car of his own, he had realised that he must abandon the chase of Majendie. Now, it seemed, he would be forced to give up not only that, but the thing from which only his obstinate determination to follow Majendie had held him.

With an effort he pulled himself together, stuffed the map and torch into his pocket, removed the key, and climbed out of the car. He slammed the door, not without a sense of bidding good riddance to the contraption which had failed him, and set himself to retrace his route.

The snow was falling much less heavily. No sooner had he observed this than it was suddenly quite suspended, in a pocket or air lock like the one he had experienced on the main road. Quickly he took advantage of it to flood the beam of his torch and see the state of the road and the sides. All shapes were swollen by the snow and their edges blurred; but he could discern on the right the deceptively shallow depression which marked the course of the ditch, banked by a blobby hedge. A couple of yards away there was a gap in the hedge, and the ditch appeared to be bridged or filled; for the line of the depression was broken by level snow which led from the lane to what seemed a field. He could strike no trees with the long beam of his torch.

He walked as far as the gap in the hedge; and there, for no

accountable reason, he stopped, and listened. Nothing broke the silence of the muffled countryside. Yet he switched off the torch and waited.

Some seconds passed. He was about to dismiss his urge to pause as a silly fancy, when he heard something; or rather, since he could hardly define a sound, he was aware that movement rippled through the stillness and was approaching him. Rapidly the movement became distinct, identifiable sounds; someone was running, floundering through the snow, gasping for breath. They were coming up behind him and to his right; therefore beyond the hedge. They were very close. When they reached the gap they would surely see him, whether they came through or not. They were level.

Brett saw the runner vaguely; alone, smaller than himself, not seeing him, staggering past the gap which led to the easier surface of the road. In a second, he realised that the runner was frightened. At the same time he recognised a certain quality in those sharp, heaved-in breaths. The runner was a woman.

He darted through the gap and flooded his torch along the inside of the hedge.

She stopped dead, and seemed to shrink together, standing paralysed like a rabbit trapped in the terror of headlights.

"Stephanie!" he cried, and leaped towards her. "Stephanie, it's all right, don't be afraid."

She turned, slowly, perhaps at the sound of her name. He halted, and in an access of self-possession held out the torch and directed it back on his own face. A cry rushed out of her, uncontrolled as a gust of wind. She stumbled forward, one hand outstretched.

"It's you," she cried, "oh, it's you, it's you!"

He clasped the hand, but said nothing. He was astonished; then alarmed; and then doubtful. Was she a decoy flung out by Majendie? It was possible. Even that would not settle her complicity. Majendie could have spun the yarn, no doubt. But she was badly shaken by something. She was clinging to his arm as if she would never let it go. What then? Experience gave priority to one explanation; reprehensible conduct on the part of a man; in this case, Majendie. Brett felt that he only now fully appreciated the services of women police; to whom, had he been on duty, he would promptly have handed any girl who confronted him with such a display of emotion.

"Stephanie," he whispered unwillingly, "what's the matter? Tell me—it won't seem so bad then."

She started to pull his sleeve, as if to drag him with her on a resumed journey. "Quick," she gasped, "quick, quick."

"Wait a minute. Where are you going?" he asked, without hurry.

She went on tugging at him, achieving nothing of the desired effect. "Mr. Majendie," she cried.

Brett's heart sank. "What about him?"

"We've got to get to the police," she almost sobbed. "Oh, do come, *quick*, please."

"I am a policeman," he said, a little puzzled.

Her hand dropped. "What?"

He wasn't shirking the issue, he told himself, as he rolled off his full name, rank and department. She had to know; and the knowledge might instil a scrap of confidence. In fact she seemed dumbfounded for a few seconds, then made to draw away from him. He let her go.

"Why?" she whispered. "Did you know? What are you doing here?"

"Does that matter? I think you'd better tell me. How can I help you unless I know what's happened?"

"All right—all right," she said, still breathlessly. "Only put your torch out. *Please*," she entreated, as he hesitated. "Oh yes, yes, that's it—just in case. Only you see Mr. Majendie, he's in a car—he was. He gave me a lift from Folkestone. And there was someone chasing him. He told me all of a sudden, and said he'd slow down round the next bend and I was to jump out and get behind the hedge till the next car had passed, then get to the police."

"But it was me all the time—"

"No, there was another much closer. I saw it go past. I'd only just got behind the hedge. When they'd gone I started to run. And then all of a sudden the torch flashed. I thought it was more of them. I thought they'd seen me and chased me. I couldn't move."

What he had heard was so relievingly different from what he had expected that Brett was only too anxious to believe it. But he remained cautiously sceptical. Even if Majendie *had* been pursued, she need be no less a decoy, intended for them, not for him. Perhaps her nerve had understandably failed; she hadn't been able to face them; whence her fear.

"Why should they follow you?" he asked.

"I thought they'd seen me through the hedge, or something. You see, I had to stop to bury the case."

"Case?"

"A little attaché case of Mr. Majendie's. He said to hide it where I'd remember the place, so I buried it under the snow just by a tree in the hedge."

Brett switched the torch on her face, disregarding her nervous exclamation. Her eyes, blinking and screwed against the light, met his with fearful anxiety and bewilderment, but with complete frankness. He absolved her from guile, and put Majendie finally in the black. Her presence at Folkestone had been providential for Majendie. Had he guessed what might overtake him? The rest of his conduct made that unlikely; nor would he have made the journey. He had simply used her in an emergency.

"All right," said Brett, "I'll take a chance."

"What on?"

Your honesty, he said to himself. "That the case wasn't filled with toffee apples. Did Majendie open it in the taxi?"

"No. Oh—have you been following us?"

"He didn't have a duplicate in the car, and change it?" he went on, ignoring her dismay.

"No."

"All right. Majendie told you to make for the nearest police. You know where that is? Not Pettinge?"

"No, the other way, back on the main road. There's a policeman's house. He could phone—"

"Yes, yes. We'll make for it. Here comes more snow, so we'd better hurry."

"Please—switch off," she pleaded, "it makes it so easy for someone to see us."

"But without a light we'll probably land in the ditch as my car did. At least, it isn't mine, it's the property of Kent County Constabulary."

"But what—what? You haven't smashed it? Have we got to walk?"

"I'm afraid so," he said firmly, moving towards the gap.

"No," she cried. "Behind the hedge."

He shook his head. "Too difficult. We want to find this policeman as fast as we can. Besides if someone did come along looking for you the hedge wouldn't give very good cover. I saw you, and I wasn't searching. We might as well use the road."

He held out his arm, which she ignored; but she moved forward. They crossed the ditch and turned right.

"There's a short cut," she said.

"In this snow, this visibility? No."

"But it's a proper road, a lane, the first on the right. It cuts off the wood corner and takes you out nearer the village on the main road. I've been along it in my uncle's car."

"All right. We'll risk it, when we come to it."

"Risk?"

"Only in the sense that a short cut is always a risk."

"But if you were behind us all the way from Folkestone," she said after a pause, "were you chasing us or the others?"

"I wasn't chasing, I was following Majendie."

"But why? To look after him, or something?"

"Purely from curiosity," he said, not caring to add that this particular bit of curiosity had first been roused by what she'd told him on the previous night.

Suddenly she stopped, and caught his arm.

"There's a car coming," she whispered, anguished.

He stood still. The snow, once again driving hard, pattered against his ears as he strained them for the sound of an engine.

"I don't think so," he said. "We'll carry on."

She didn't release his arm, although they were now almost running.

"If they did come along before we could get off this road," she panted, "what would we do? Are they—are they dangerous?"

"Perhaps to Majendie."

She uttered a cry of distress. "And he made me run away. I do feel awful."

"Spare yourself," said Brett drily. "He made you run away with the best part of the danger."

"What?"

"The case."

"That?" Her voice squeaked in her astonishment. "What's in it? Not something that might blow up?"

He couldn't help laughing. "Can you imagine Majendie coming within a mile of a bomb? But you've no idea of what might be inside?"

"No, of course not—oh look! Here's the lane."

Brett swung the torch beam to the right. It was dazzled back by the swirling snow, but he could see the hedge and the ditch turning at a sharp angle.

"Right then," he said.

They turned off the road and ran plodding on in silence for a time. The ground rose, not very steeply, but continuously, covered by snow which lay in most places about six inches deep, and greatly clogged them, whether they kicked through it or pulled their feet out at each step and plunked them down again. The fall drove almost straight on their backs; yet such were its eddies and flurries that flakes were constantly blown in their faces. To try to puff them aside was exhausting, but an instinctive reaction; so it was to brush them off, even though this left the face wet and stinging.

Brett was warm, but he wondered about Stephanie. Her coat was thinner than his, and she had been out longer. He looked at her. The yellow raincoat was soaked to darkness, and the flat semi-slippers which he'd noticed at Folkestone were no longer beige but black.

"What are you wearing under your coat?" he asked.

"My shop clothes. The grey dress."

He groaned. "What ineffable vanity made you wear that coat and those shoes in such weather?"

"I didn't know I was going to have to do all this."

"But even if *all this* had never happened—oh, never mind.

Shall we stop plunging along in this tiring fashion? I'm not sure that it's so much faster than walking."

Their amended pace, although slower, was as brisk as conditions allowed.

"How long before you met me had the car passed you?" he asked.

"No idea. It was all a dream. You know, time didn't count."

"And when you jumped out of Majendie's car and hid behind the hedge? You'd hardly consult a watch in such a crisis, but did you happen to see—"

"No."

There was a considerable pause.

"Do you do murders?" she asked suddenly.

"Not as a rule," he said, taking her meaning after a bewildered moment. "I have encountered one or two."

"What then? Robberies and burglaries and that? I suppose that's bad enough."

"What do you mean?"

"Well, it's such a ghastly job, isn't it? Daddy says in the end all detectives get the same as the greasy people they mix with."

"Oh?"

"Yes."

Brett marched on in silence.

He was aware that such an opinion was widely held; it had never before been uttered point blank to his face. Of course. Stephanie's tone had been not waspish but indifferent, almost blithe. He was fairly sure she hadn't intended him to infer a personal slight from her generality. She had simply demonstrated once more the thoughtlessness of the self-centred, and somewhat spoilt child. And he wondered, that a remark so little to be heeded should have stung him; as, momentarily, it had.

The snow had begun to lighten; and in a few minutes ceased to fall. He saw trees on either hand. Stephanie was walking very close to him and as he turned to her she halted.

"What is it?" he asked.

"I'm afraid," she said in a very small voice, "we've come the wrong way."

She sounded so worried that he hadn't the heart to give vent to a fraction of what he was feeling.

"We shouldn't come into the woods at all," she went on. "The proper lane would cut them off on the left."

"Well then, that's not so bad," he said, trying to sound cheerful. "We missed the right lane and took a later one which goes through instead of skirting the woods. I expect it'll join the main road in the end."

"But there isn't another between the one we should have taken and the road. Nothing goes through the woods."

"Well—where are we? You know this region."

"But I don't, not all that well. We only come here for Christmas, or sometimes a weekend. And then not really here but Pettinge."

He wished she had said so before offering to take them by a short cut. "Shine the torch down," he said, "I'll look at the map."

He glanced at the sides of the lane, which had narrowed to little more than a path. The trees, bounded by neither bank nor fence, grew right to the edges, which were as straight as if they had been ruled.

"I think this is a private road," he murmured, feeling his pockets for the map, "or a ride cut through a plantation. That means there should be a fairly large house nearby. All to the good."

His search for the map ceased to be casual.

"Have you lost it?" asked Stephanie.

"I suppose so," he muttered, after ferreting fruitlessly for a few moments longer. "I must have dropped it right back at the car, slipped it past my pocket instead of into it. Well, it doesn't much matter. We can't be lost in a county like Kent. We're bound to come to a house of some sort fairly soon. We'll go on."

They plodded forward.

"I'm going to switch off the torch," he said. "Shut your eyes for a second or two, and you should be able to see well enough when you open them."

"All right. But why? So's not to waste the battery?"

"Partly." He switched off. "You find it light enough?" he asked after a few moments.

"Oh yes. But it doesn't ever seem quite right, does it, in the snow? Everything seems closer, or further, you can't tell which. Somehow not in its right place, and settled."

"It's because the natural direction of light is reversed. The earth shines, and the sky is dark. So there are no shadows. I suppose they're cast upwards and absorbed into the night."

She shivered. "Let's hurry. I don't like these trees."

"*Quem fugis—*"

"What's that?"

"A bit of Virgil," he said.

"Don't you know any more?"

"*Quem fugis, a, demens? habitarunt di quoque silvas.*"

"How nice it sounds. What does it mean?"

"Go on, try. Surely you can do *quem fugis*?"

"Who flies?"

"What? *Fugis.* Are you deaf? And *quem*, accusative."

"Well? Oh, you fly. Why do you fly?"

He sighed. "*Whom* do you fly. Now—*a, demens.*"

"Well, *a*'s the same as *ab*. From, away from. Whom do you fly from?"

He stared hard at her. As far as the uncanny light allowed him to see, there was no trace of her minx-like smile.

"It just means ah," he said calmly, "or oh, if you like. Go on—*a, demens.*"

"Oh—oh, demon?" she hazarded.

"*De-mens.*" He carefully separated the syllables. "What's *mens*?"

"A month."

He groaned. "Mind. *Demens*, out of one's mind, crazy, insane."

Stephanie began to laugh. "Oh, you should have been one, especially with that nose. A Roman, I mean."

"My nose is *not* Roman. Much too long and sticks out too far."

"Well, it has a bumpy bridge. Brett—"

"You didn't see that on a coat," he observed, rather absently.

"There was a note in your kitchen from your wife—at least, if that's who Christina is."

"You read it through?" he asked. "Estimable."

"I was going to say," she went on in a much abashed voice, "I think we're coming to a clearing."

"I've seen it for some time."

He stared at the white space which broke the line of trees some twenty yards ahead.

"Tell me the rest of the Latin," said Stephanie irrepressibly, skipping forward. "Or can't you?" she burst out laughing.

"Ah, crazy, whom do you fly?" he began.

Stephanie stopped dead in her tracks. Brett's voice failed him.

A man had stepped silently from between the trees and was waiting at the end of the path.

Brett forced himself to carry on walking and speaking. "Even gods have lived in the—"

———

About him in the dark he heard voices swelling and fading; close and distant at once, like the voices of sailors talking in a railway carriage as one nods off to sleep. He listened apathetically for a while. Then he thought that he couldn't be in a train, because—but how did the sailors fit in the cabin? He drifted back to sleep.

Hours later, drowsily half opening his eyes, he saw the sheets and white quilt of his bed bumping away into shadows. Of course, he was not in a train, but in bed in the nursery. He felt the chill of a fever sweat, heard the hiss of the steam kettle in the grate. He could see the fire, but not look at it, because it was so bright that it hurt his eyes. Wavering, elongated figures blotted out its light from time to time. They were his mother and the nurse, and the murmuring voices belonged to them, and they were talking about making him well. He closed his eyes and fell asleep.

When he woke he felt ghastly. He was ill, no doubt of that. Although it was still dark, Christina must have had to get up. The lamp at the dressing table nearly blinded him when he looked to see her vague shadow moving as she dressed and brushed her hair. She must also have brought the wireless into the bedroom, because someone else was talking, a man. That would be the first news bulletin of the day.

He moved his head, and immediately felt sick. Alarmed he lay still, waiting for the qualm to subside. He became conscious that the bedclothes touching his head and hands were soaked with cold sweat, and tried to push them away.

But he found that he couldn't move. He puzzled over this for a few minutes before the explanation came on him. He was paralysed.

He opened his mouth to call Christina. Nothing happened. He couldn't make a sound. His locked throat cracked with no effect. Then he realised to his despair that Christina had gone; worse, that she had never been there. He had imagined her. She didn't know that he was lying ill and dumb and helpless. He was abandoned.

Suddenly he felt a splash on his cheek, and the wetness of it ran down his chin. Something hard was pushed against his mouth, something cold trickled between his lips. Instinctively, he swallowed. The cold turned burning hot. Brandy.

With a shock he woke up, groaning in relief. He had been, as so often, dreaming on the verge of nightmare. He was lying not in a fever sweat but in snow. He was not paralysed but bound. In slipping down the crevasse he must have struck his head and knocked himself unconscious. They were treacherous, these Bavarian Alps. Nor, of course, was he abandoned. Christina and Reinhard had gone to fetch help. Now it had come. That explained the brandy, which must have poured from a cask at the neck of a St. Bernard dog. He had been brought to himself by a dog, and like—like someone he'd heard about recently. And already the rescue party was at work. He was being hauled, strapped, to safety. There was the blinding searchlight, there the roaring engine of the helicopter—the helicopter—

The helicopter. Brett opened his eyes. The world spun as if he were perched on the spoke of a circus wheel. It settled. It seemed larger than was right. That, he realised, was due to the angle from which he was seeing it. He was lying on the ground. And he knew that he was at last truly awake. He knew where he was, what had been done to him, and what was happening. He was being dragged by the shoulders, bound, through a snowy clearing in a Kentish wood, having been hit on the head from behind his back—by the same hand as had hit Beddoes?—as he came along the path between the trees. He knew who had brought him to it. Stephanie.

Nausea rushed out of his nightmare to seize him. "I'm going to be sick," he said, weakly. He was still dragged backwards. "Stop," he gasped, "I mean it."

Someone, with last minute speed and humanity, rolled him face down in the snow, lifted his shoulders and held his head. Everything flew from his consciousness except the horrors of vomiting. It was so long since he had been overwhelmed by them that he had forgotten how even without pain and without danger that most distressing upheaval prostrated the sufferer. There was nothing left to him but his sickness. While it lasted, life faded, time was suspended, yet an end was inconceivable. But of course it did end; and as the spasms abated the first of his returning perceptions was of a pain insistently chiselling into the back of his head. Sight, hearing, and touch came back in confusion. All he wanted was to lie down and be left alone in the dark. Shuddering, he turned his head, seeking somewhere to lean it. He found someone's arm, and let it lie on that.

He was rolled back, propped against someone's knees. Whoever it was, they had a clean handkerchief with which they wiped his mouth and let him blow his nose.

"Give us," said a man.

After a moment's fumbling, someone passed the scent of brandy near Brett's nostrils. Feebly, he shook his head. "Water," he whispered.

There was a short silence.

"Here," said the same voice.

Brett felt a cold substance held to his lips. He opened them, and received a rather clumsily administered mouthful of snow. After the first surprise and the first convulsive shiver had passed, he let it melt gratefully down his throat.

"Duster come down too rough," muttered the voice.

"He didn't know who it was."

"Come down too rough all the same. Here."

Brett was offered, and took, a second mouthful of snow.

"You'll make a bloody Niagara of this," went on the first voice. "Can't you see they're sniffing round us? Why not sling while you can?"

"Must be a coincidence. The police wouldn't be so stupid."

"You don't know them like I do. You don't know just how stupid they can be," said the first, morosely. "Here, have a drop of this now."

This time Brett did not refuse the brandy; which was, however, withdrawn so quickly that he swallowed only once.

"What are you doing?" demanded a third voice. "What the hell are you doing? I said get him in."

It was not until the newcomer spoke that Brett fully awoke to the contrast which existed between voices one and two. Voice one spoke in a low rapid mutter with which years of duty had made Brett familiar. Voice two, and now voice three, proclaimed without fault a middle-class origin and environment. For the pinched speech of the newcomer, moreover, Brett felt a dim recognition.

"Stan here thinks the police are stupid," said two, "and he's nursing this one like a mother. Yet he's breezy because he thinks they're on our tail."

"I know what I'm doing," said three. "There can't be anything wrong or we'd have had a message. D'you want your share?"

"What share?" said the Stan voice. "Don't forget we've got nothing in our hands but trouble."

"That's not our fault. We did our best. Anyway she may help us yet. Come on, now, bundle him in."

"Why don't you listen to me?" Stan expostulated. "I've been in it since I could spit. You want to leave this old bath-chair, no one's going to find it here for days, weeks. I ask you—two cars, bonnet to bumper. Sticks out a mile to the rawest flat in the force."

"Not at Christmas. Parties—"

"We ought to stick together, all in the fastest."

"Too much load. And what could look more suspicious than a car bulging with men?"

"Not at Christmas," retorted Stan sulkily.

"All right, that'll do. I'm in charge. You can get in the back—of *this* one—with them, Duster driving. Tim, drive for me, will you? Get a move on, Stan, time's short. Pick him up."

"Here, give us a hand, then," cried Stan, "as if he's a fairy!"

From a slight distance came a rejoinder that Brett could not make out.

"Smug little cocky little tits!" muttered Stan with venom. "Public perishing school! Hey, Duster! Give us a hand."

Someone, apparently new, approached. Together they took hold of Brett as nurses heave up paralysed patients. As he swung up, the snow jumped into a glare under two dazzling beams.

A noise like a waterfall broke the stillness. So much, thought Brett, for the rescue searchlights, the helicopter. He gathered from the third voice that there were two cars, although he couldn't see a second set of headlights. As he pondered this problem, his shoulders fell from four hands to two. One of the men went to his feet. As he bent to pick them up, the lights lit his face.

Wacey, said Brett to himself, without surprise. That was the Stan, the old hand at the game. And Wacey, not the other, had held his head and had given him handkerchief, snow and brandy. Why such tenderness? He was no friend to Wacey. An explanation was trapped somewhere inside his brain, like a fly buzzing against a window pane. He thought it had to do with the tense of a verb. Dreamily he started to conjugate *tollo*, his childhood's favourite. *Tollere, sustuli, sublatum*—he was indeed being raised, to the accompaniment of a good deal of grunting. His right side was bumped against some sort of frame.

"Shove up, zany, can't you?" he heard a strange voice say roughly.

His shoulders were jerked, slipped, and fell. His head cracked against a wall. Through the dinning pain that seemed to fill his skull he heard a groan, the sort that greets a fumbled catch in a Test match.

"Mr. Nightingale!"

Someone at the far end of a speaking tube called his name.

"Hullo!" he answered.

"Shut up."

"Dear fellow—"

"Shut up, I said."

Two Whitehall lines had crossed, he concluded, and waited for the speakers to sort themselves out. Nothing happened. He felt himself hoisted into a sitting position, his support being soft yet curiously uneven. He opened his eyes. He was in a small dark cabin. In the corner of the far side a pale face was suspended in gloom, like an old tenth-rate painting in an historic mansion. He stared at it in silence for a while.

"The portrait of a blinking idiot," he said finally, and closed his eyes.

He was woken by cold air blowing on his face, and knew at once that he was much better. He moved his head experimentally; although it still ached, it was clear. He didn't feel at all sick. For that he supposed he had to thank the ministrations of Wacey, which, however unorthodox, seemed effective. Hesitating between the conjugations of *ministro* and *efficio*, he opened his eyes.

Wacey was sitting opposite, looking not exactly at him, but vaguely round about his ears, with the uneasy ambience of an old lag.

"Better?" he muttered.

Brett nodded. "Thank you," he said.

He had no fear that Wacey would not extract from these two words the last dram of significance. Without further verbal clarification he had understood the nature of Wacey's solicitude. It was an insurance policy taken out against the obviously not far distant hour of reckoning. No doubt he hoped Brett would remember to credit him with the instalments of brandy and snow. And indeed, he would.

Conscious of a certain strength in his weakness, Brett looked out of the open window. *Open*—Wacey was laying out really heavily.

They were driving at fair speed along a reasonably wide but unlit road. No snow was falling, although it lay thick on verge and hedges. The major hindrance to traffic which had threatened appeared not to have developed. Brett remembered bitterly the drift in the lane to Pettinge. But that had been in a tiny side road; and if he hadn't pulled to the left he still might have been—

The phrase warned him that any line of thought which

followed would be quite futile. If in the circumstances he could do nothing but speculate, he must at least speculate on the future; on where, for instance, he was being driven in this large square car. The second car—naturally he hadn't been able to see the lights, as he was being carried back towards them. The second car. She had said only one passed—but why was he still rashly giving consideration and credence to her? He shut his eyes quickly. The only certainty of his awakening was that she had made a fool of him. He wished he had stayed in the hazy world of the nursery, the Bavarian Alps and tricky conjugations.

It occurred to him to wonder how Wacey could be sitting opposite instead of beside him. He stared, and saw that Wacey's seat was pulled down from the division which shut off the driver. Next to Wacey's was a similar seat, occupied by the person to whom belonged the suspended face he had seen before, but whom he now perceived to have a body also. He turned his head to the right. The fourth corner too held a passenger. Brett peered at him. The car was lit only by reflection from the snow outside; but that was strong enough.

"Majendie," said Brett.

The figure stirred, in an oddly restricted way.

"Nightingale—my dear fellow! How do you—"

"For heaven's sake!" said Brett, disgusted. "Don't you think you could peel off that skin of hypocrisy? Haven't we passed the price-cutting stage?"

"Shut up," murmured Wacey, in tones of mild reproof.

"Look here," protested Majendie energetically, "can't you hear the man's beside himself? Surely you're not so blunted to humane—"

"Shut up," said Wacey more firmly. "Now cut it out."

Brett, who had turned his head away from Majendie, promptly turned it back. In a second he divined the reason for

Majendie's clumsy movement, for his present stillness, for the extraordinary language in which his subordinate addressed him. Majendie, propped in the corner of the back seat, was bound like himself.

His diagnosis of the situation, of the whole affair, disintegrated; and, in a minute or so, was reformed to a new pattern. Of course Majendie had been pursued, and not only by him; that much was right. Majendie had underestimated the shrewdness of his associates. They had reached the same conclusion as Brett. And now Majendie was hoist with his own petard. As for Stephanie, Brett's opinion of her was modified only to the extent of wondering where, in his new disposition, she belonged; to the main party, or to Majendie.

"Where is she?" he asked, almost against his will.

No one answered. Nor did Wacey tell him to shut up, as Brett had expected.

"Where is she?" he repeated.

"I shall never forgive myself," said Majendie suddenly, in a voice quite unlike his own.

"Oh, stop this unutterable birdseed!" cried Brett impatiently. Suddenly he was stricken with apprehension. "What happened?" he asked, quite oblivious of her lies and defection, remembering only her smooth neck and straight back and the golden hairs caught up on her shoulder.

"Poor child—she did so struggle and cry. I'm afraid—"

Majendie broke off. The car had slowed and come to a temporary standstill, its engine running. Without a word Wacey leaned forward, opened the door a little, slipped out, crouching, into the ashy twilight, closed the door soundlessly and was gone. The whole thing was over in a few seconds; and the car went forward.

Brett could only gape. He was reminded of the first crime

he had ever seen, when, as a child, shopping with his mother in a crowded store, he had turned round suddenly and caught a man in the act of whipping a bale of gingham under his overcoat. Then, as now, he stared, his brain numbly doubting whether he had really seen or only imagined. He never knew. Then, as now, he was silent. The man had slipped unobtrusively away.

But why, in this case, was there such silence? That Majendie shouldn't care was not surprising, but what about the man on the other seat? He was surely one of them. He certainly wasn't another bound victim, for his hands lay limp on his knees. He and Wacey might have come to an understanding. Wacey's departure had been too furtive to suggest that it was to schedule, that it was anything but the *slinging* advocated by him in the clearing. Then had he gone so furtively as to pass unnoticed?

Brett looked at the man on the pull-down seat. His face was turned towards the door by which Wacey had left. His stare passed blankly through the window. He sat, as he had done all the time, quite immobile.

Something in the face and posture struck a response from Brett's memory. At the same time he was aware that what had so clearly shown him the face, and the hands on the knees a minute since, was a brighter light. There was a car following them, another about to pass in the opposite direction; and they were travelling faster. From the increase in traffic and speed, Brett gathered that they had turned into a major road. At that moment he heard a whisper from Majendie.

"Mr. Nightingale—do you hear me?"

"Yes," said Brett.

"You understand what I say?"

"Of course."

"Forgive me, dear fellow. You've said such odd things—I

wondered if you were quite yourself." Majendie rushed this out in one breath. "But—we can speak freely if we don't raise our voices above this—you understand—"

Brett could half see Majendie, his head turned away from the pale man, trying to convey by grimaces that before such a one reticence was superfluous.

"What is it?" he asked.

"This is the main Dover road, you see, A2," hissed Majendie. "Do you think—traffic seems reasonably heavy—could we make a bid—"

"At this speed? Tied?"

"But perhaps manage to attract attention? If we're over-taken again—the window's open too—"

"Where's Stephanie?"

"Miss Cole? In the other car. It went ahead of us, but I can't see it at the moment. You're thinking it would be scandalous to leave her. But if we could get away to tell the police, have that car stopped—unless you know it couldn't be done. Poor child, poor child!"

So she was of the main party, Brett thought, with no more than a passing gibe for his wasted anxiety. Naturally she went with the Kellett's or Geoffrey side of the business. Yet by the very name Brett was reminded that without her help he would have known nothing of Geoffrey, the cellars, Majendie's collection. She had mentioned the dressing case itself—

"*Did* you give her a case to hide?" he asked.

"But of course—didn't she tell you?" Majendie sounded astonished.

"She did. But I've been thinking that was simply flimflam to distract the great gullible while he was led into the love nest."

"My dear fellow! Do you suggest that she's one of them?"

"Why not? You gave her the case—all right, but suppose she just handed it to them as they passed on the road?"

"Then why did they come on after me and nearly smash us all to pieces forcing me to stop, and, and, *and*, dear fellow, rip up the seats and the carpet looking for the case?" Majendie was quite triumphant.

"Of course," murmured Brett, "the second car. It's yours."

They did have only one. She had been truthful in that, thought Brett, avidly seizing the fact. "And that's why the seat feels bumpy. Did they draw into the wood to strip the car in seclusion, do you know?"

"Yes. One of them, the man Tim, knows the country. So do I, of course. It was Colonel Waring's place we turned into, by a side drive. Acres of woodland. That glade used to be the site of a Palladian temple of love—odd you should call it a love nest just now—I thought you must know it too. The colonel had it pulled down some years ago. An excellent spot for *their* purposes. Only two approaches, ours and yours."

"Yet you can believe that we stumbled into it by chance."

"But if you'd seen her fight and kick—despite the gun—"

"The what?"

"Yes. I was too cowardly, I fear. I knew someone was coming, so did they, of course. One of them was posted at the main entrance, another at that path. I rather gather he saw a light at some distance. He called the others—there are four—or there *were*—and one of them went into the trees while he—Tim, it was—waited at the edge. I heard you coming. The path seemed to act as a sound channel, and in the open air, I think, one tends to raise the voice unawares. Then I heard Miss Cole laugh—I didn't recognise her voice, but I knew I should call out to whoever it was. But as I say, to my shame,

I couldn't do it. The man Geoffrey, you see, pointed the gun at me."

"Geoffrey!" Brett remembered the familiar third voice.

"So they call him. You think that perhaps you know him?"

"No," said Brett cautiously. Majendie might or might not be quite ignorant of Geoffrey. "It's a fanciful name for a thug, that's all."

"But you know, they're an ill-assorted bunch. Two of them I imagine to be typical underworld characters—the one who jumped out and our present driver, Duster, they call him. I don't know whether—"

"Occupational," said Brett drily. "He *dusted* me a little while ago."

"A professional—slugger? Then thank God he's with us and not with Miss Cole."

"And the other two? Perfect gentlemen? I think you said Geoffrey pointed the gun. Look! We're turning off A2. Do you know where we are?"

"Let me see—we joined the road when that fellow left us, just past Barton, you know, my own home. We've turned north-east—towards Adisham, would it be, I wonder, or the next road up—"

North-east. Brett felt an incredulous flutter of hope; that after all his disappointment and despair he was being carried to no other place than Richborough. He recalled the arguments in the Palladian love glade. Wacey guessed, scented trouble with a professional keenness. The others, overconfident, were sailing ahead. Admittedly, they were the Hampstead people, who had pulled off two robberies important enough to boost anyone's confidence. But clever as they were they lacked both the cautionary sense developed by long practice and the inside tricks which distinguish professional polish from amateur zeal. The instinct of the professional underworld on meeting a policeman, in Brett's experience, was to slip quietly away; and if the worst came to the worst, and they laid him out, to pelt off at full speed, leaving him to recover as best he might; certainly not to encumber themselves with him.

Public perishing school! The vindictiveness of Wacey's words lingered. These people were not only new but foreign, not of the pure criminal stock, outsiders. Was that why information had at first been so difficult, and why Pink, at last, had informed with such obvious relish?

"Do you think," said Majendie suddenly, and hesitantly, "that there's any question of—a threat to life?"

"Probably not to mine," said Brett callously. "It's a deadly sin to kill a policeman, and even they know the wages of sin."

"But that unfortunate child?"

"I doubt—" Brett stopped. He had summed up his whole thought on Stephanie. "As for you," he went on, "well—you should know your chances. What have you done to deserve it?"

"Done? But I've done nothing, nothing!"

"Then why did you cut the price of my cameo?"

The question flew out of his mouth like a bird; and was succeeded by a silence.

"Look here, dear old fellow," Majendie eventually whispered in a very nervous voice. "Difficult, I know, in the circumstances—medical attention—but take my advice— lie back—relax, you know—try to keep calm—"

"Come off it!" Brett, furious, felt the brazen tongue of Beddoes leap into action in his own mouth. "Stop pouring out that padded cell syrup. I'm absolutely ice cold sane. Did you or did you not tell that pomaded monkey to soften me up with a slice off whatever I wanted?"

"Good God, sir!" hissed Majendie, evidently stung out of his concern. "If by that offensive term you mean Mr. Emmanuel, certainly not."

"In your position, why not speak the truth?"

"Do you have the effrontery," cried Majendie, his voice swelling in outrage, "to mistrust my word to my face."

"I trust no one," said Brett.

"Indeed, I imagine suspicion and cynicism, if not congenital, are soon ingrained in a policeman. A sort of occupational disease."

The conversation languished. Brett, looking out of the window, wondered how many people whose good will and friendliness he accepted without question really regarded him with discomfort and distaste.

After a minute or so he became aware that Majendie was mumbling indistinctly in his corner.

"—sincerely—forgot myself, I'm afraid—allowances—head—ill—unsettled—"

"Don't bother," said Brett, "it's true."

There was a pause.

"And you must realise," went on Majendie, with much more assurance, "that not every item of stock is known to me. Describe this cameo."

Because it seemed so pointless, there was no point in not complying. Brett told him.

"Sixteen, seventeen, pounds or guineas," said Majendie. "Possibly a little more or less. Not more than twenty. Of course, immediately after the war it would have been another matter."

Brett was silent. Emmanuel had let Majendie know how much he had cut, that was all. It was true that Majendie sounded uncommonly convincing. But his plausibility had never been in doubt.

"Why not take an independent valuation?" he suggested now.

That was easily said. They had first to get out of their present plight.

"But what put such an idea into your head?" Majendie persisted.

What indeed! Or rather, who. Brett said nothing. Nothing was safe. What layer on layer of deceit and probing and sifting wouldn't they unfold—they, including Majendie. Majendie, he noticed, had showed no curiosity as to what had brought him on the scene in the first place.

He only just managed to keep back a groan. He didn't know what to think, and his head ached. He was beginning to feel the strain of being tied; since Wacey had left the car he had been struggling to free himself, but his efforts succeeded only in pulling the bonds tighter or in making his wrists swell. Above all he longed to be with someone he could trust. The forbidden name nearly broke surface, the unmanning image which would set him fretting and sweating, and reduce his brain to worse, if possible, than its present uselessness.

Quickly, to divert the thought, he looked at the third passenger. He sat as before, mute and still. A phrase echoed in Brett's mind—*shove up, zany, can't you?* Zany. A person not to be reckoned with, not to be heeded, before whom anyone might talk freely; a sitting target for a bully. The Simpleton in *Boris Godunov*. That, Brett thought, was the likeness he had almost reached earlier, when Majendie had interrupted. The Simpleton, without hope, had no choice but to endure suffering and mockery. Yet the Simpleton was not a fool. His sly dreamy sallies made Tsar Boris blench. He had no illusions of a new life under a new leader; he went on singing of the grief and toil that was the life of Russia.

Russia. Exactly, thought Brett, feeling quite calm in spite of his sudden enlightenment. He stared into the corner. Dimly he could see the third passenger's straggling moustache.

"Ivan Ilarionovich!" he said softly.

———

"What!"

The crude exclamation shot out of Majendie with unaffected force. Except to note its sincere astonishment, Brett ignored it.

"Ivan," he repeated, "Ivan Karukhin! Do you hear me?"

"A Karukhin," whispered Majendie, "*the* Karukhin!"

"Don't you understand?" Brett went on. "But I was forgetting—of course you do. You've lived in England all the life you can remember, forty years, nearly, in Bright's Row. You're British, on paper. Ivan!"

He paused. No one spoke.

"All right," said Brett, "it doesn't matter. You needn't say anything if you don't want to. I can tell *you*. I know it. I know about the parents *you* never knew, the dissipated father, the delicate docile blonde mother who bequeathed you all three qualities—and perhaps an affectionate nature. That would have been doomed from the start to wither. You had no one to love, only one to fear. Yes, I know about the grandmother. Grown people feared her when she was sane, so how much more a child when she was mad."

"Mad, would you say?" said Majendie.

"Oh, not helplessly, pitiably—certainly not pitiably. Not in that state of mental conflict that's never, by any means, resolved. She was just mistaken in external circumstances, deluded. As if the Leningrad firing squad wanted *her* for a triumph!"

"Persecution mania—"

"How real was that fear? It was there in degree, of course, in that she went to the extreme length of mewing herself up in Bright's. Mad, if you like—but also, I think, lazy. Start to *work* in middle life? Never!"

"But she needn't have worked," cried Majendie.

"Pride, both chronic and acute. Sell the only remnant of her consequence, the one tangible assurance that she was truly a princess? No, no, no. Any dolt, any tradesman, can have money. Only Princess Karukhina could have had that particular diamond rivière, that antique heirloom Louis something snuff-box, and so on."

"She sold some," observed Majendie.

"'Formerly the property, I believe, of Princess Irina'—wasn't that so? And perhaps some pieces she'd never cared for." Brett paused. "Oh, she kept you, Ivan, just!—till you could keep her. You were an investment, that's why she bothered to make you safe by naturalisation. Besides, she was always careful of servants. And you served! I know how you passed your childhood, struggling with cheap shopping, buying and eating God knows what—enough, that I've seen your adult breakfast!—dressed by the chance of a neighbour's pity, ill washed, sickly, a plant in a cellar. Healthy children recoil from feeble ones. Asthma must have kept you out of rough games. Besides, didn't you live with an old witch? The other children in the street probably saw her at the window, even though she never came out—a fact which would make her all the more terrifying. School? I know—years of dimness near the bottom of the class. *Lacking in confidence*, that's what would have gone on your reports. And where would you have gained confidence? From work? Independence? What a hope! She stopped selling the odd brooch and sucked up your miserable pittance instead, your reward for fifty weeks a year of grind in a stuffy office in the smoke of a main-line station—"

"But my dear fellow," Majendie objected, "it's up to each one, after a certain age to look out for himself, assert his rights—"

"What had there been in your upbringing, Ivan, to give you to think that you might have rights? Did you think so—at that stage? Such mental agility as you were ever to possess developed late, and no wonder, when your mind and your youth were stunted by habit and fear. Besides, you found, quite early, an opiate. Who taught you to drown your sorrows? And how did you manage it? Perhaps you kept her in the dark about wage increases, which you must have had eventually, and spent the extra in the pub. In time, I suppose, the extra wasn't enough. You drank and spent more, braving whatever she said to you, because your loneliness was getting unbearable and the rebuffs of childhood and the overlookings of the office had made you fight shy of approaching people, because your life offered no other pleasure, nothing, in fact, but squalor and boredom from which drink gave the easiest escape. In the end not even the pub could blind you to the enormous rift between other people's lives and yours. But by then, although you may have wished to clear out of Bright's Row, you couldn't afford to. Oh, your wages went up and up, especially after the war, but so did your drinking. The more clearly you perceived your situation, and the longer you reflected on it, the more despair and frustration you had to drown. You knew you'd never command better money, you couldn't keep what you had, and you'd no capital. I think you tried to get some—that *Greyhound Express* in your wardrobe, was that a sign of your attempts?—but you were unlucky. So your life was slipping away, eaten by routine—office by day, pub by night—when one afternoon, not so long ago you came home sick."

Brett paused. There was still not the slightest response from Ivan; yet on the chance of his hearing and understanding, Brett was determined to go on. He glanced through the window, but could make out nothing. If they *were* heading for Richborough, he had to be quick; it wouldn't be long, even allowing for their speed being reduced by snow, before they were there.

"I think that must have been the first time," he went on, "that you were *sent* off duty, as opposed to taking sick leave for a whole day. If you'd been in the habit of arriving unexpectedly, she would always have locked the door, and in those days she didn't. So you walked in. And the trunk was open.

"You'd never seen inside it. As a child, perhaps, you'd asked and been fobbed off—what did she say, family papers? You'd grown up with the fact that she rarely left the room, so I suppose it never occurred to you that there might be a reason for it, other than her peculiarity. How could you guess that anyone living in penury could be in possession of such a treasure as they were unwilling to let out of their sight? Well, of course, on that afternoon you *saw*. What was she doing? Disposing the contents round the room? Curtains drawn? Wearing the jewels perhaps—parure of emeralds, Siberian, and diamonds, Brazilian, displayed on a crumb-spattered shawl. Re-creating an era."

"An unexceptionable pastime, my dear boy," murmured Majendie.

"Thereafter she locked the door," Brett went on, "not, as Mrs. Minelli thought, to keep out the Red peril, but to make sure no one else interrupted her as she counted out her treasures. She didn't bother to hide them from you, there was no point in it. You saw them again, many times, came to know them by heart, in tiny detail, as a child knows a fairy story. In time, unawares, you grew to love them—at least one of them. But that you didn't discover till too late. In the meantime your first thought was that the contents of the trunk would provide you with the capital you'd despaired of. If you stopped to think before you spoke, I suppose you concluded that she was madder than you'd realised, too mad to appreciate the value of the trunk. But you did speak. You *explained* its value—what a moment!—and suggested that she sell.

"Of course she wouldn't. But how it must have shaken her to discover that you weren't so stupid, that through those years of apparent submission you'd been daring to nourish ambition! Perhaps she also discovered with what virulence she hated you, though she may have known herself well enough to have recognised that already. *You* must have been surprised when she disclosed it. Callousness you'd met, as a child, contempt, when you were drunk—that is, more or less permanently, at home. Why did she let you become so familiar with the treasures, even when she knew you coveted them, when she'd gone to such lengths to keep their existence secret? It was as if she said, 'Here, then, look your fill, babble it to the world. I'm not alarmed—who's going to heed the boasting of a sot?' And didn't you find that true? *Prince, bleeding poet.* Scorn, derision, you knew, but not to be hated."

"And what, would you say, was the cause of that hatred?" said Majendie. "One sees, of course, a certain—"

"Ivan, you were the son of *her* son," Brett cut in quickly, "that obstinate fellow who had dared to cross her, and of the daughter whose docility she despised even though she expected it. You embodied them. You embodied her past failure, mistakes and follies. She couldn't put them out of mind because she couldn't put you out of sight. She had cunning enough to know that she depended on you, reason enough to know what had made you as you are—heredity, aggravated by her upbringing. She'd made a rod for her own back, but like most people in that position, she wouldn't admit, beyond the first secret acknowledgment, that it was true. Most people find a way out. She did. Your existence was a reproach, she turned it into an offence. To save herself from hating herself, she hated you."

Brett stopped. Lights shone outside the windows, at the side of the road and behind coloured curtains in houses. They were passing through a considerable village. He saw a pub, a chapel, a filling-station, a weatherboarded wall with posters on it.

"Wingham, or I'm much mistaken," whispered Majendie, "on the Canterbury-Sandwich road, you know. Heading for the coast, do you think?"

"Easy to understand your feelings," Brett went on. "She'd injured and insulted and finally began to torment you. Didn't she, after her first searing refusal to sell, constantly reiterated, take a malicious pleasure in setting out the treasures in your presence? Didn't she say that you were not to be her heir, would never touch so much as a bead of it? Perhaps she told you she'd already made the will. She hadn't, but how could you know? All you knew was that alive she deprived you, dead, she deprived you. And you were in despair, divided between drinking yourself into oblivion and trying to think of a way out.

"You had one brilliant idea—to have her certified. You consulted a doctor, perhaps even a solicitor as well, only to find that it wouldn't work. What about stealing the trunk? It *could* have been done, despite her almost continuous presence. But you knew you'd have had a very short start before she discovered the loss, you knew she'd have notified the police, that you'd be the first suspect. Even if you managed to hide, how could you have hoped undetected to get rid of the pieces? Of course, you thought of killing her. The trouble was the same—inevitable discovery. You could think of nothing that didn't end in that. So more arguments, more drink, more despair—until, one night in the Oak Tree, you met Stan Wacey."

"The one that jumped?" asked Majendie with interest.

"The one that jumped," said Brett. "How did he come to be in that pub—by chance? Most unlikely. *You* didn't take the initiative, Ivan, I'm sure you didn't. You'd been marked, and Wacey spoke first, working you round to the subject of your inheritance—easily done, with the aid of several pints— thence, to the trunk."

"Good God! The risk—"

"Wacey lives by risks. Of course he was careful, cagey. When he was sure you were ripe for it, he pointed out that it would be better to make sure of part than to lose the whole. He suggested you sell not the trunk, but the information of its existence, and share the money proceeding from its professional dispersal with whoever helped you to lay your hands on it. You fell. I expect he pretended he wasn't interested for himself, and screwed a few pounds out of you as the price of passing the information to the right place. Anyway, he must have arranged a second meeting, probably not at the Oak Tree. Vanbrugh Street? Never mind. You went. He introduced a nameless friend, an interested party, whom you regaled with each beloved detail of the treasures. You explained the difficulties—her close watch on it, the bolted door open only to you or Mrs. Minelli. They were quite confident of finding a way round all that. *You* were to be in the clear. Everything would happen while you were at work. They fixed a date, a long time ahead, to give them time to organise. After the event you were to receive the first instalment of your money—what, fifty in advance?—but I expect they told you it was useless to stipulate for a definite final sum, as they couldn't say how much they'd make. And in the circumstances you had to be content."

"Honour among thieves, they say, I know," said Majendie, "but it does seem to me that such a haphazard way of setting about a dangerous enterprise, such a lapse of time between promise and performance, would give rise to doubt—"

"Doubt! Ivan, you must have been exhausted by constant change of mood. Mostly you feared that they'd steal the trunk in their own time, leaving you helplessly cheated. And if nothing worse, you'd still lost the money you'd been induced to part with. But then you'd dream of the approaching liberation. The trunk gone, she'd have lost her sting. She could either stay in Bright's and rot while you went off to better yourself, or come with you—on *your* terms, and with you holding the reins. What if she raved to the police? Who would believe that anything had existed outside her addled brain? Your sudden affluence? Lucky bets, accumulated savings—it would have been troublesome to disprove. But in fact, Ivan, you, and they, were in a false position from the start. There was someone who had—not *seen*—but received part of what was in the trunk. Mrs. Minelli. Your grandmother gave her an ikon and a brooch, long before you'd seen the treasures. But of course you knew nothing of that, so, in good time, you went to the doctor for sleeping tablets."

"Hm! No cheaper, and certainly less anonymous, than a shillingsworth of aspirins from a strange chemist," commented Majendie.

"You went to the doctor partly from habit, partly in the muddled and mistaken belief that an authentic prescription would establish the innocence of your purpose. It was carelessness on their part to leave you to get the tablets. Anxiety made you overact, draw attention to your sleeplessness and yourself. However, on the twenty-first of December you went to Vanbrugh Street, to hand them your key. I imagine Mrs. Minelli often had to let you in, so she wouldn't necessarily conclude that the key was lost, nor ask questions. And on the morning of the twenty-second you made breakfast earlier than usual, putting into your grandmother's cocoa an extra-large dollop of condensed milk and a crushed dose of sleeping tablets."

"An overdose, I suppose you mean?" said Majendie.

"Well, yes, but not such a colossal one. A long heavy sleep was the object. You forgot, Ivan, that tough and indestructible as she must have seemed to you, she was an old ill-nourished woman. You saw her to sleep—that's why you'd had to start early—and went off to work, where for once you forced yourself to your colleagues' notice, even attached yourself to one of them at lunch. As at the doctor's, self-consciousness—"

"My dear fellow! Surely an understatement! One would be expecting at any moment a call from the police."

"Not more than a little. You knew what they were going to do—unfasten the string from round her neck, open the trunk, transfer its contents to their bags, lock it, put the key back on the string and retie. With luck she wouldn't discover for a day or two that the trunk was empty. And as there *was* no alarm during the day, you went in the evening to the Vanbrugh. What met you? Long faces and no money. Remember you'd told them in detail what to expect. Remember they were experts. One piece they'd specially looked forward to getting their hands on, a piece they wouldn't have to break up, for which an unscrupulous private collector would pay thousands. And it wasn't in the trunk. They said you must have kept it for yourself, or it had never existed. You swore good faith, utter ignorance, amazement, innocence. That didn't help as regards money, but apparently it convinced them you were speaking the truth. They suggested, I think, that she might for some lunatic reason have taken it out and hidden it about the room, or even in other parts of the house, and that you should go home, give her another dose of tablets and look for it while she slept. You hesitated. They pointed out that if she discovered the robbery before you could find and get rid of the missing object, she'd be able to show it to the police, who'd be far more willing to believe in vanished glories when one of them remained. So you went back to Bright's.

"You saw from outside that the window was dark. You were startled but not alarmed. You concluded, I imagine, either that the tablets had made her too drowsy to light the gas or that the first sleep hadn't yet broken. You went upstairs, knocked and called. There was no answer. You tried the door. It opened. You went in, struck a match, lit the gas, looked round—that must have cost you an effort! But there she was, lying peacefully in the bed. You crept across, stared for a minute, and realised that she was dead.

"The shock of that corpse was like the blast of a bomb, it blew you out of the house and down the street in a whirling panic. You didn't know where you were going or what you were doing, only that she was dead and you were done for. You must have raced down Upper Street or the High until— what? Asthma—your breath gave out. When you *had* to stop your brain calmed a little, fell into its strongest habit. You wanted to feel better, you wanted solace, oblivion. You went into the Derby Arms.

"Yet, you know, if you'd kept your head, or at least regained it, and had gone to *them* with the news, I think they'd have thought it a worthwhile risk to notify your doctor. She was very old, quite likely to die in her sleep. With luck you would have pulled through without an autopsy. After all, there would have been no immediate trace of motive, crude motive—"

Majendie stirred, as if about to say something; but he evidently thought better of it.

"Conscience—better say, awareness of guilt,—was your stumbling block, Ivan," Brett continued. "You *knew* you'd caused her death. You were sure that discovery and punishment would follow, that any evasion would be only temporary. Money, the treasures, *they*, the police—all irrelevant. For you, life was finished. You were as good as dead. But from force of habit you drank on. You had moments of lucidity, and in one of them you suffered a pang of regret for what you'd lost, lost even in life, let alone death. I said you loved it unawares. How could you help yourself? It was beautiful. Oh, a toy, a glittering extravagance—some people would say its beauty was meretricious, which is all very well for those who've been able to pick their way through the purest art in the world. But to you, in Bright's Row, it was pure. Ice and frost and stars! That's what you said to the man in the pub. And he called you a bleeding poet."

The car bumped, tipping Brett sideways. Recovering himself, he leaned his head against the back of the seat. He felt very tired. His arms were aching, and powerless as ever, bound at elbow and wrist.

"No use, Ivan," he said wearily. "You rolled out of the Derby Arms, through the dark, till you came to the canal, and like a true Russian, in you jumped. No use again—you were followed. My friend, a noble soul, a sergeant, Jonathan Beddoes, he pulled you out in the name of humanity and the Metropolitan Police. But they were following you—all the evening since you left the Vanbrugh. They didn't trust you, they wanted to see that you really went to Bright's Row, and if not, where. When you ran out of the house, they guessed why. One stayed, I think, to report developments. The other tagged along behind you. They had to get hold of you, before you babbled. They might have shut you up in a quicker, rougher way than they did. That's how I've guessed you kept to Upper Street, too bright and busy for you to come to harm—not that you could have known or thought of that. They, the one of them, watched you into the Derby Arms. That's where Beddoes came in. I think they saw and knew him, sent for reinforcements, a car, perhaps, to lurk nearby. When you came out, you all lolloped along behind each other like a string of dogs, you, Beddoes, them. When you jumped, they let Beddoes rescue you, then knocked him out and took you away. And what they've done with you since, and why they've kept you, I don't know. You certainly couldn't tell them where to find what was lost. You didn't know then, you don't know now. In any case, they soon had a good, if vague, idea of their own, which I believe I unwittingly suggested to them."

"My dear fellow, are you sure you—"

"You see, unbeknown to you, she was at work in the last couple of weeks irrevocably to deprive you of the trunk. Did she sense the approach of death, without necessarily guessing that it would be unnatural? Even if that's too fanciful, she can't have failed to notice a change, a strain, in the atmosphere. If you overacted before indifferent strangers and colleagues, how much more in that brooding presence! She decided to make haste. She summoned to Bright's Row, on your pay day, so that she could be reasonably sure that you'd stay at work, a well-known jeweller.

"Of course, she wasn't conscious of the enormous irony of her choice." Brett paused. "The man was also a collector, a lover of jewels, a connoisseur of Fabergé's work. He instantly coveted, or loved, your own beloved. It was too easy for him, trusted as he was. What excuse he offered I don't know, but he took it away with him, just that one star of the collection. Perhaps he even paid a token sum. We found no cheque, no cash, but it's not impossible that she slipped out and put it in the bank. I said, you remember, that one of *them* probably stayed to watch the house on the night of the twenty-second. They had their reward. They saw the police cars, they saw me. They followed me on to a bus and off it, and watched me knock on the jeweller's door. Enough. They put two and two together. They watched *him*. But he foxed them, almost to the end."

"*Almost?* My dear fellow, if there were not this nasty doubt of living to enjoy it, I could justly correct that to *entirely*. That, in fact, would be the lesser of my corrections. I understand your suspicion—indeed the exposition of your thought was interesting—if rather in the Pharisee line—"

"What?"

"I mean, in your attitude to the Princess. You condemn—but how would you have come through the Revolution in her place? Is it possible to feel no pity for her undoubtedly deranged mind?"

"Is it possible to feel none for its victim?" Brett meant to say this louder than in fact it came out.

"Well, well—we each defend our own generation. For I think, despite the differences wrought by character and environment, that you and Ivan Karukhin are much of an age?"

"He's five months younger. Oh, damn! I didn't mean to say he. Ivan—"

Brett broke off what he was going to say. He was aware of change; as when a sauce, stirred for long minutes over a slow heat, all at once starts to thicken. The pace of the car was slower than it had yet been, and paradoxically it was this slackening which told him that events were speeding to a crisis. The car had reached a tiny hamlet, no more than a cluster of cottages breaking the monotony of the whitened hedges, and left, between them, it turned off the road into a narrow, ill-surfaced lane.

"What do you think?" whispered Majendie. "Should we make a move, at any stage, an attempt to get clear? Because, you see, I've been following our course—and I'm afraid we're heading for nothing but the Stour."

To his annoyance, Brett began to tremble. He knew it was due to relief and exhaustion, but that only infuriated him the more.

"Turned north before Ash," Majendie was going on, "never a sight of it. Now we've swung left. Difficult to judge speed and time, but if we'd kept on the main road through Ash we should have been at Sandwich long past. I'm sure of that. I say—do you see? He's put out the lights."

Brett did see. They had driven through a gap in a hedge, where a gate either stood open or was gone, and had stopped short beyond it. There was now only a low bank to their left.

On the right, level whitish land stretched without a break until it melted into darkness.

"There's the other car!" exclaimed Majendie. "Rear lights about twenty yards ahead—and I say! There's a man coming towards us."

As he spoke, their driver got out, leaving his door open.

"Nothing," said Brett quickly. "Do nothing, say nothing. Leave it to me. Here they come—and won't they be pleased!"

The door beside him opened. He saw that the second man was not Geoffrey, so presumably Tim. For a couple of seconds the two men gaped, silent and aghast, at the empty seat beside Ivan. Then the driver began to swear.

"Where is he?" demanded Tim sharply, ignoring Ivan and addressing himself to Brett and Majendie.

"Slipped out," said Brett coldly.

"Where? When?"

"Some time ago. How should I know where?"

There was a pause.

"No guts, these people," said Tim at length, with something of the chill of an upper civil servant condemning a lapse into humanity. "Why the devil didn't you keep an eye on him?" he reproached the driver.

"Got them in the back of my head, have I? How could I know he was going to jump?"

The driver was furious. He leaned forward, seized Ivan's arm, pulled him out of the car and shoved him into a sitting position on the footboard. "Why didn't you shout, jelly boy?" he said, whacking the back of his hand so savagely across Ivan's face that Brett was only just quick enough in shooting out his bound legs to break Ivan's backward fall.

"All right, all right," said Tim. "Don't waste time. It can't be helped. His loss, anyway. Come on, Bright Eyes. You're going to change places."

He hooked his arm under Ivan's and pulled him to his feet. Still supporting him, he walked away, followed resentfully by the driver.

"A Karukhin!" Majendie sounded appalled.

Brett said nothing. He stared out of the window, trying to pierce the distance, to discover a shack, a clump of bushes, anything that might give cover. But were they, in fact, at Richborough? Majendie could be wrong; and he hadn't named a place, only the river, and the Stour marsh was wide. Brett was turning to question him, when his eyes were caught by something between the cars.

Three figures, slightly foreshortened in the deceitful snowlight, were coming towards them, the two outside holding between them a third, much smaller, whose legs trailed like a helpless drunk's. Who now? thought Brett. A name flashed through his head. It was absurd, impossible. But he looked hard at the approaching trio. It was true. He let out an exclamation, not knowing what.

"What is it?" cried Majendie.

"Stephanie," said Brett.

The door was pulled open. Tim came first, backwards, carrying her shoulders. Duster held her feet. They set her down quickly on the floor, and went without a word, Tim making his way out by Majendie's door and slamming it.

"Mr. Majendie!" she cried. "Oh, Mr. Majendie!"

"My dear, dear girl, thank God! I thought you might be hurt—you're not?"

"No, no, I'm just tied up. Oh, Mr. Majendie—" She burst into tears.

Brett was amazed by his detachment, so cool that it verged

on boredom. He saw that he had been wrong, and Majendie right, about Stephanie; yet the understanding brought him no relief nor remorse. All his anxiety, all the events of the afternoon, seemed thin dreams. He heard Majendie uttering sounds such as emanate from a hen house on a sunny afternoon, quite well calculated to soothe. He saw and felt that Duster having gone back to the wheel, had started the engine and was driving them slowly out to the open space on the right. From their lurching, lopsided progress, Brett gathered that the snow covered no longer so much as a track, only rough grassland. With an effort he brought his attention to bear on the inside of the cabin.

"It's all my fault," Stephanie gulped. "That man in the other car, it's Geoffrey. He has lunch with me. I didn't know—I told him you had a collection, that you were coming down here today—I'm sorry. I didn't know—"

"Of course not, how could you?" Majendie consoled her. "Don't worry, my dear, we'll soon be out of all this, quite safe and sound. Look, here's Mr. Nightingale in the corner— haven't you seen him? Or perhaps you haven't had time to learn his name—"

"You! I thought they'd left you behind," she cried. "Oh, are you all right? Did they hurt?"

"They didn't tickle."

"How odd your voice sounds."

"Yours isn't quite natural."

"I can't help it—I'm not really crying, it just keeps coming."

"Of course, of course, we understand," said Majendie, reproachfully, as it seemed to Brett. "You've been magnificent. You're sure they didn't hurt you?"

"No, oh no. Just kept on asking and threatening—about the case, of course. I just pretended I didn't know what they were talking about, and so there was nothing they could do.

They're raging mad, but they're in a hurry to get somewhere. I don't know why they've stopped here."

"You see, dear fellow?" said Majendie triumphantly.

"I see," said Brett. "They didn't talk between themselves at all?"

"Only just now, before they brought me over. Someone's gone—"

"We know."

"Oh. And that man who hit you—it was a sort of sausage he used, did you know?"

"A sock and sand, I suppose, or rubber."

"Well, he kept on saying he didn't like it, but Geoffrey—" Her voice quivered. "Geoffrey told him to drive further out—this car, I suppose—so that you shouldn't see. The driver said you'd see anyway and you weren't deaf either, but Geoffrey made him. He said to mind the ditches. That's all. Oh, where are we?" she concluded miserably.

"Inexplicable as it seems," said Majendie, "somewhere about Richborough, by my calculation of time, direction, and so on—hullo!"

The car had stopped. And Majendie had named the name, thought Brett. Could he, at last, fully acquit him? But that must wait. If this was Richborough, where were *they*, Kent? Where in this white wilderness could they hide themselves? *Were* they hiding? *Someone had blundered*, he thought with a shudder. He fancied them diverted by a false message, its authenticity not questioned till too late. Or was it conceivable that his plan had at the last minute been overridden, Superior Wisdom having insisted on a concentration at the point? Or had they even thought that in such weather the meeting would surely be cancelled?

Duster, the driver, got out and closed his door. He was

going away. Brett watched him lumbering and slipping, trying to hurry over the treacherously pitted snow.

"What now?" asked Majendie quickly. "He's left the engine running. Why?"

"Batteries? No, we've no lights to drain them. Ready to get away quickly, perhaps. Apparently they don't intend to leave us here. I thought they might."

"What's happening?" asked Stephanie.

"The driver's gone," explained Brett, realising that from the floor she could see nothing. "Can you move your fingers?"

"No. They tied my hands flat out, and the strap goes over the fingers." She sniffed audibly.

"Something to be said for Daddy's family saloon, isn't there," said Brett.

"I think," said Majendie, "I can move mine a little—right index and thumb. What do you want?"

"If we can, to shift along the seat and turn back to back, so that you can untie my hands. I think we should get out now, if possible."

Brett worked himself along till he met Majendie.

"Awkward, dear fellow," said he. "We can't turn exactly back to back or we shall fall off, I fear. Wait now—can I reach your hands?"

Brett felt a fingertip brush his left thumb.

"Perhaps if we leaned back," suggested Majendie. "The angle of separation—"

"Wait!" exclaimed Brett, starting. He was staring all the while out of the window. About a hundred yards away two pairs of headlights had been switched on.

"Stephanie," he said. "Did you see a third car back there?"

"Not see it, but there was a van, they said so."

"A van! Only *one*?"

"What is it?" Majendie was asking. "Shall I go on?"

"Could I bite it?" Stephanie suggested.

"I think it's too thick, my dear." Majendie checked his slow feeble plucking. "Do you hear anything?"

Brett listened. The engine of the car thrummed quietly. Above it, literally above it, another and much more powerful noise was making itself heard.

"There is a railway across the marsh," said Majendie.

Brett shook his head. "That's not a train."

"An aeroplane, perhaps. Something from Manston. I should have thought the weather too bad for them to be up. Up, did I say? He seems to be rather unusually low. Not in difficulties, I hope."

The noise was now indeed ear-shaking, a great spattering roar, as if a titanic coffee mill were grinding coarse.

"That's not an aeroplane," shouted Stephanie at the top of her voice, "that's a helicopter."

Brett heard Majendie's excited squeaks. He didn't listen. If Kent were there—if, if!—they must start to close in now, or they'd miss the best of the bunch. The helicopter could rise in a trice, leaving bystanders staring up like the apostles in a picture of the Ascension.

"Quick," he breathed, "quick, quick—"

The uproar ceased abruptly. The sound of their own engine was, in comparison, scarcely noticeable. Brett blinked. The helicopter, gently clumsy, had lowered itself into the beams of the headlights. For a moment or two it hovered and shifted sideways, rotors still whirring, like a huge out-of-season dragonfly quivering over a pond. Then it settled. Immediately the headlights were switched off.

"Has it crashed?" Stephanie sounded frightened.

"No, landed," said Majendie, who had abandoned his attempt to free Brett, and was himself gazing out of the window. "Inconsiderate, dear fellow, eh? to turn off the lights at this point—good God! A Verey light!"

From the darkness, beyond the cars, a scarlet flash streaked into the air, and even as Majendie gasped the marsh turned chalk white. In the middle of a glaring lake of artificial light the machines stood up like rocks. Between them, a knot of men held for a couple of seconds the frozen poses of a tableau. Then they scattered like dropped peas, some to the cars, a couple to the helicopter.

"Police!" cried Majendie in exultation. "My dear boy!"

"Too late," whispered Brett. The blades were spinning, the engine broke into its clattering roar. The two men were barely at its side as the end-heavy creature lifted itself with a little jerk off the ground.

"Too late?" shouted Majendie.

"It's up," Brett bawled back. "We're all right, though."

He looked at the helicopter. The beam of a searchlight clung to it relentlessly. He frowned. The helicopter was not rising, nor flying forward, nor hovering, but bucking about as if caught between the gears of all three motions. An abrupt leap carried it in their direction. Brett bumped back to his corner and pressed his face against the window. What else was happening he didn't know. He had eyes for nothing but the helicopter. It was low, very low. He could only suppose that it was trying to dodge out of the searchlight. But why not get away? Registration letters—

With a sudden lurch it swung out of his sight. He glanced quickly back at the marsh. One car was gone, the second, incredibly slow, was only now moving away. All at once he was aware that Majendie was shouting with a new note into his ear.

"What?"

He turned. The inside of their cabin was bright from snow and the lights. The din of the helicopter was deafening. Brett looked into Majendie's stricken face, and without hearing, knew what would happen. For an instant he felt a presence overhead, crushing and inimical. It struck, a punching downward blow on the front of the car, smiting its nose into the dirt. The rear lifted and bounced back. Brett and Majendie were flung from the seat against the division and collapsed helplessly over Stephanie. The car slithered, rocked, and was still.

Brett, propped at an angle with the floor by the heap that was Majendie and Stephanie, bent his knees, pushed with his feet, arched his back, and thus managed to stand upright, at least, as upright as was possible in the car. Tears streamed down his face. His nose was running, warm and fast. He had hit it on the division as he fell. He licked his upper lip, and recognised the tinny taste of blood. He shook his head, blinked, and looked out. The helicopter was going away over the marsh, barely clearing the ground, in a series of hesitant leaps, like an old lady jumping puddles. Out of the corner of his watery eye Brett saw the flicker of a distant bonfire. He looked round, straight ahead, through the driver's compartment. The flames were darting not from the horizon but from their radiator.

He felt as if his jaw and lips were frozen, but he knew he would have to make them work. He shuffled his feet precariously, turned, and bent to the open window. His voice came, cracking horribly. He yelled. Although the helicopter was further off, its noise still raged. He spat out a mouthful of blood and turned back to the cabin.

"Majendie!" he shouted.

"What is it?" Majendie, evidently too shaken to shout, was only just audible. "I can't get up."

"You must," bawled Brett. "The car's on fire, the engine—"

A wail from Stephanie interrupted him.

"Get your free fingers to the door catch on your side," he went on, shouting. "Fall out and roll away. Steffy, listen—listen! When he's gone wriggle and bump until you fall through the door. Keep your head up as you fall. Then you roll too. And shout all the time."

There was no need to tell them, he realised, himself beginning to howl like a demoniac. He dropped to the back seat and tried to swing his feet against the door. They couldn't kick with any force from such a position. He stood up again, aware of Majendie's furious heaves and struggles to get his back to the opposite door. The flames were shooting up quite fiercely. Of course the police assumed that an unmoving car was abandoned, and now that it was burning they would even more think so. Brett tried to strike his helpless hands against the door catch. The old hearse—if they didn't get out quickly it would be a hearse, all right, he thought. *Old.* A frightful possibility struck him.

"Where's your tank?" he shouted to Majendie. "Back or front?"

"Front!"

Brett flung himself against the door. The tank couldn't be broken, or it would have gone up by now. It must be just the carburettor. But very soon—a gravity tank—petrol would be pouring out, pools of it, and a continuous jet of flame from the broken pipe—

"There's a tap," he heard Majendie yell, "driver's seat—otherwise the tank may blow—full at Folkestone."

Brett gave a desperate shove, and the door flew open. He fell out of the car. "This way!" he croaked to the others.

Someone touched him. The door had been opened, not

broken by him. Someone clumsily, and with labouring breath, dragged him clear. Twisting his head, he looked up.

He opened his mouth, and a whisper came out.

"Ivan!"

His astonishment melted. "The tank," he said urgently. "Switch the tap off, Ivan, down by the steering column."

Ivan hesitated.

"The driver's wheel," cried Brett. "Or take the knife from my left trouser pocket and cut me free. Quick."

Ivan fumbled.

"*Left!*" shouted Brett in despair.

Ivan had the knife. With movements painfully slow he cut Brett's arms free. They were stiff and numb. Brett worked and shook them as Ivan sawed through the rope round his ankles. Feeling it give, he pulled his feet apart, snapping the last few strands, scrambled up and ran weakly round the boot.

Ivan ran with him.

"No," cried Brett, "the others. Pull them out, well away, both of them, then free them. Hurry. I'll help you when I've done."

Ivan pulled open Majendie's door, Brett the driver's. The bonnet was blazing in patches, where puddles of petrol had formed. Even inside, Brett could feel the heat of the flame. He bent down and groped for the tap, low, to the right of where the driver's knees would come, where he had himself seen a tap on a very old car. The searchlights didn't reach so low. But he found it, and turned. If it worked, if the whole thing wasn't stove in, it would cut off the flow of fuel, and the fire would be confined to the puddles. He straightened his back, and saw that the key was still in place. He switched off, although he didn't know that it would now make any difference.

He jumped out of the driver's compartment, and staggered. His knees were shaking; his shins ached as if he had just got past a bout of influenza. A trickle of blood still oozed from his nose. Wiping the back of his hand across it he went through Majendie's door. Stephanie was gone, and Ivan, terribly short of breath, was heaving Majendie by the shoulders along the floor.

"All right," said Brett, "I'll do it."

He stepped crosswise over Majendie to replace Ivan at his shoulders; lifted them, and dragged Majendie backwards out of the car.

"My dear boy!" Majendie kept repeating, in a badly shaken voice. "My dear boy, if that tank had cracked while you were down there—it's an old car, and the metal is most likely not quite—I don't like to think—"

Brett held him up while Ivan cut him free. "All right?" he asked.

"Yes, thank you, yes. Quite sound in limb, if not in wind. No, I can stand, I won't be downed. Went through worse than this in '15, dear boy. See to Miss Cole."

But Ivan had already released her. She jumped up as if she'd been bound with nothing more painful than cobwebs; but she was crying.

"Oh, Mr. Majendie," she sobbed, flinging herself at him and seizing his hand. "Your poor dear old car!"

"There, my dear, don't cry." Majendie made a supreme effort, in spite of his trembling voice, to be quite himself. "I'm not a pauper, you know. Poor old lady, she's keeping us warm—although, I believe, the fire's contained now. Mr. Nightingale's work, that. It's all right, my dear, all over now."

Brett looked round for Ivan. He was walking rapidly away, almost running.

"Ivan!" cried Brett. "Ivan, wait. Please."

Ivan turned, and stopped. Brett ran towards him, slipping in the snow, saving himself in a final lurch only by catching hold of Ivan's arm.

"My knife, please," he said, holding out his hand.

Ivan stared at him. Reluctantly, with a nod which seemed to show that he very well knew why he was asked for it, he put the knife into Brett's hand. The blade was still open.

"Thank you," said Brett, "thank you, thank you." He hesitated, looking down at Ivan, who was so much smaller. "I'm sorry," he went on. "Everything I said—I did know you were listening, but I wanted to try to show you that I saw, or thought I saw, how it all came about. I'm sorry."

Suddenly Ivan spoke; a soft rapid sentence of which Brett understood not a word. It took him a couple of seconds to realise that Ivan must have spoken in Russian. How could he possibly answer that? He ran off in his mind his brief Russian vocabulary. Tsar, kremlin, soviet, niet. He was silent.

So was the marsh. Outside the windlike roar of the fire the hush was broken only by brushes of the real wind. The helicopter had gone, the cars were still. And through the silence came a shout.

Ivan started. Brett, nearly falling, discovered that he had been leaning on him.

"No," he said, holding him back; for he had made to run away. "Where would running take you? Only to them. It's hopeless. The ditches? No, no, you won't do that again. You did something even harder, and that with a clear mind—came back when you needn't have, risked being caught—no, made it certain—all for three strangers. Then don't go. Just clinch it, finish it, prove it— to Majendie who knew other Karukhins, to them, who'll see the only one that's left. Don't try to run away. Go to meet them."

He stared down into Ivan's face. Behind them Majendie's voice rose in a quavering shout.

"They're coming," said Brett. "They'll be here in a minute. Don't let them just find you, Ivan, go to meet them. Quick, go now. Show them, show them—please."

Without looking at him, Ivan took two steps forward; three. He stopped. There were men running towards him; a lot of men.

Brett tried to will him to go on. But he knew he couldn't do it. He hadn't even strength to keep trying. He gave up; and a whole phrase of Russian slipped into his mind. It was foolish, extravagant, inapposite; the title of the opera in which, very shortly, he would be playing the part of a professional buffoon.

"Lyubov k trem Apelsinam!" he said.

Ivan turned. "Oranges? Love of three *oranges*?" he said in a tremulous London voice. He shook his head—pityingly, as Brett realised. "Sometimes you say things make me think you're daft."

He turned back, and walked towards the approaching police.

"Schoolboys?" interrupted the Superintendent.

"Yes, sir," said Beddoes, with a poker face and back. "Grammar schoolboys, sir, I believe."

"Well, never mind, sergeant. Go on."

"Well, sir, there was no incident till about two miles past Charing, when the Majendie's brake, followed by the plain blue van from Kellett's, pulled into the forecourt of a public house. One of Mr. Majendie's men was seen to get out and go into the lavatory at the side of the court, whereupon both men left the blue van and entered the front of the brake, which immediately drove off at speed. At the time, both vehicles were thought to form one party, but all the same it seemed remarkable that one should have been abandoned in view of our belief that they were both loaded with valuables." Beddoes glanced swiftly at Brett. "Accordingly our nearest car proceeded to give chase, which, owing to the considerable speed necessarily maintained, soon became obvious. The brake began to be driven recklessly. As a result of radio communication with the County Constabulary, patrols were diverted to intercept, and in swerving to avoid them on their appearance, the brake overturned at the side of the road. Fortunately the occupants escaped with bruises and shock. When apprehended, the men from the van volunteered that they had been heading for Richborough, and confirmed that a helicopter was expected there at six-thirty, giving the exact location of landing. They had been ordered to follow and seize the brake because it was believed that it might contain an article of value, which they were to deliver at Richborough. The information was immediately communicated to the County Constabulary—"

"Who thought that as he'd had such a let-down over the van he'd been chasing," broke in the Superintendent with a smile, "they'd restore his spirits by letting him in on their party. It's all right, we got the O.K. from your end." The Superintendent smiled again. "Our Inspector, you see, he knows that marsh like the back of his hand—local chap. The plan was for him and another to lie up in the nearest drainage ditch—the place is netted with them—wait for the landing, send up a flash for lights, and dash forward to secure the helicopter, leaving the rest to the ring closing in. Of course, when we'd been given the exact spot we were able to take up much tighter positions than we'd expected, which was a great improvement, and we had cars at the road points to stop any escape on wheels. When we picked up Sergeant Beddoes here, the Chief suggested that as he'd been responsible for that helpful bit of information, he might care to replace *our* Sergeant—you know the idea, big gesture, Christmas, and all that. Plenty of time to get him here from Charing, so that was soon settled."

"What was?" asked Brett.

"Why, that he should nip up to the helicopter too. And so he did. The plan didn't go quite without a hitch. They couldn't run as fast as they'd have liked on account of the snow. Isn't that so, sergeant?"

"Yes, sir."

"And as the pilot hadn't left the machine he was able to start up quickly. They just managed to heave themselves aboard as the thing was airborne. Then of course this chap Hayes, the pilot, showed resistance, and in the scuffle the inspector took a knock that laid him out, which was particularly unfortunate as the whole point of choosing him had lain in his ability to take the controls in an emergency. He belongs to the local flying club."

"Beddoes!" said Brett, feeling slightly weak, "what did you threaten that pilot with?"

"I didn't threaten him, sir," said Beddoes, with angelic voice and mien. "I'm afraid, sir, I had to incapacitate him."

"How?"

"With a kick, sir, in the first place. Then I'm afraid I had to hit him when he went down. On the chin, sir, and the nose, but not to breaking point. Then, sir, I sat down at the controls. I made a few experiments—"

"Yes, I know!"

"I'm very sorry, sir. I didn't mean to hit the car. And finally I managed to bring the machine down."

"Very creditably, considering everything," said the Superintendent. "Of course the undercarriage was completely buckled, but what's that, after all? The jolt brought the inspector round. He switched the rotors off for us, and the engine—yes, what is it?"

A head and a uniformed shoulder were poked round the door. "The girl's father's just arrived, sir."

"Oh, yes. I'll be out in a second." The Superintendent turned to Brett. "If you'll excuse me, I must go and soothe parental agitation. She seems a nice girl."

"Very nice," said Brett.

The Superintendent went out and closed the door.

"Boil me!" said Beddoes in a low and pithy voice. He sat down on the edge of the table. "A very nice girl. Boil me! I never get these jobs with nice bits of blonde crackling thrown in. No, no—send the sergeant chasing down the Dover road after a load of perishing Christmas puddings, that'll do for him."

"Beddoes, I'm sorry. I thought, about that brake, what they thought, except that I counted on the lot and they on Majendie's party piece. And I don't remember that you put forward other suggestions. Weren't you surprised?"

"Surprised! You should have seen it. Not just the puds—pâté, sausages, fruit, turkey, cigars, enough to feast a battalion, all rolling over the road. The doors burst open, you see. Prize picking in that ditch, I reckon. There'll be tramps passing the sign the length and breadth of England. On the way here they were telling me that Majendie's Christmas and New Year parties are famed in the district, especially at Nackington."

"Nackington?"

"Traffic H.Q. Apparently his guests by the time they leave, have usually formed an idiosyncratic interpretation of the highway code, and I can well believe it. Of course, I thought of picking a pud apart to see where the diamonds were."

"Aren't you satisfied yet? Isn't it enough to have made me

feel like Prometheus? Yes, there was snow, as on the mountain peak, and a descending eagle—"

"I didn't feel like the king of the birds, I can tell you. How I love terra firma! I say—" Beddoes hesitated. "Would you mind if I had a cigarette?"

"Don't be ridiculous," said Brett astonished. "What's seized you?" He watched Beddoes take out the cigarette and a match, and wondered at the length of time he took to get a light. The flame danced like a midge round the cigarette end; because, as he at length realised, Beddoes' hands were shaking.

"You know what you'll be given for all this?" he said thoughtfully.

"A putty medal. Sooner have a cheque."

"Promotion," said Brett.

"Boil me! Ps and Qs all the time."

"Yes, and I shall be sir, sir, sirred, by your successor. How exceedingly strange!"

Beddoes puffed out a ribbon of smoke. "The pilot, Keston Hayes. *Is* he American?"

"No, he affects the accent. And his real name is Maurice Wright. He's British, so we can gobble him up. But you haven't mentioned *the* point about him. Have you forgotten, or did you never hear it?"

"What?"

"That he used to be Guzmann's personal assistant."

"He did? Very interesting. No hope of tripping up Guzmann himself—"

"But no harm in trying. The Hampstead people—how odd, to know largely who they are."

"*They're* odd, if you ask me. Not quite the thing, as the old bird would say."

"Who? Oh, Majendie. Do you know what he called your flash? A Verey light."

"Distinctly passé."

"At least it's honourably passé. Anyone who's tasted trench warfare has a right to have spent the rest of his life in a jewel box. Besides, he came through that episode in the car with colours flying, and look how he's borne up since. So less of the old bird, Beddoes."

"But that reminds me—you've heard that this wasn't the usual exit for the stuff—sorry, the stolen property?"

"No?"

"The man in the van told me. By the way, I suppose you have sent home to get them to see to Kellett's? All right, I only asked. Well, the heli was a last resort, to clear it as quick as poss in view of dangerous complications. I suppose they meant Mrs. Karukhin. As a rule they go by discreeter channels."

"They'd have done better to stick to them," said Brett. "I'm sure it wasn't for want of advice from Wacey."

"He skipped off, I gather. *Sauve qui peut*. Not the philosophy of Ivan the Terrible—no, can't very well call him that since he's donned his halo. Strange! Blood of the Boyars, I suppose, and so on. Well, no again, because I think they were a shower, mostly. How did he manage to get to your car without being stopped either by them or by us?"

"You forget his capacity for being overlooked—and underestimated. Besides, *how* he came is nothing to why. Can you make smoke rings to order, Beddoes, or are they quite fortuitous?"

"Just a chance. You haven't seen Ivan since they locked him in?" said Beddoes slowly.

Brett shook his head.

"Oh. They asked him that. He said he went back because he had a friend in that car."

"But he'd never set eyes on any of us till today! Good God!" Brett jumped out of his chair. "Surely we're not going to have to start thinking about Majendie again?"

"Oh, boil, bake and fry me slowly!" said Beddoes. "Sometimes I wonder—" He stopped, sighed ostentatiously, and shook his head.

"What?" said Brett. "Well, what did he mean by it?"

"Forget it. He's not too bright, after all. And you know the old bird—Mr. Majendie's really all right, don't you? Well, stop worrying. More to the point," said Beddoes with a sly look, "to ask why he decided to give himself up. After all, to face a murder charge is no sneezing matter."

"Ivan may get off with manslaughter. I think he should."

Beddoes whistled, with slight tremolo effect. "He'll need a good counsel."

"He'll get it."

The door opened, to readmit the head and uniformed shoulder.

"Your call to London, sir. Will you take it in here?"

"Yes," said Brett. "Thank you, put it through."

"Ah," said Beddoes, sliding off the table, "this is where I get a chance to take a look at the crackling!" He stubbed out his half-smoked cigarette, and loped, grinning, out of the door.

Brett picked up the telephone. "Hullo!" he said. "Christina?"

"Yes, darling, what is it?"

So casual, so unconcerned! Of course, it wasn't at all late, as he was thinking. She wouldn't have been expecting him.

"Nothing really," he said. "I'm in Canterbury."

"Good heavens! Do you remember that awful hot day we were there? Red-faced girls all sweat and haversacks combing their hair in the cathedral. Oh darling, won't you be able to come home for tomorrow?"

"Yes, oh yes, tonight. What's special about tomorrow?"

"Brett! Christmas."

"Oh, hell and damnation!"

"What's the matter?"

"Nothing, nothing," he said hastily, "I was thinking of something else." He was thinking of the cameo. "Did you enjoy the cantata? I didn't want to wake you this morning."

"Oh, it wasn't bad, except that they had a moo-cow instead of an alto, and of course *he* had no idea—"

"Chris," he interrupted, "you know that saying, He that toucheth pitch—"

"Oh, there was nothing wrong with her pitch, it was just those awful lowing scoops, and the way she bludgeoned the phrases."

Brett sighed. "Listen Christina. Does it ever dismay you to think that you're married to a detective, all scum and suspicion?"

"What? Brett—are you all right?"

"Of course I am," he said impatiently, "how else could I be talking to you? I only asked a simple question. Isn't there a simple answer?"

"Yes. I mean, yes, there is. Oh darling, the kettle is boiling over, I can hear it. I must go. You come home as soon as you can—you'll get your answer."

"But Christina—"

"*Zu neuen Thaten, theurer Helde!* Goodbye!"

Hearing a decisive click at the other end, Brett put down the telephone. He stood still for a minute or so, pleasantly anticipating the promised answer, not for one second entertaining the idea that it might be given verbally. Then he went out of the room; meeting the Superintendent a few yards along the corridor outside.

"Ah, there you are," said he, "I was just coming to see if you were ready to go. The thing is this. It appears there's some property of Mr. Majendie's buried behind a hedge on the road to Pettinge. We were quite willing to send someone to pick it up, but Miss Cole seems to find it difficult to describe the exact position—she hid it, you see—and as she's got to go to Pettinge in any case it's been decided to let her do the finding. Between ourselves I think she could have told us well enough, but she wanted just this to happen. Well, why not please her? She's been through a lot. Don't you agree?"

"Entirely. Where do I come into it?"

"Well, Mr. Majendie seemed to think you'd be interested in coming too. Don't if you'd rather not, of course, but if you like to—"

"What transport do we have? Can I take Beddoes?"

"Yes, yes, by all means," cried the Superintendent expansively. "There's Mr. Cole's car and mine, plenty of room for all. We're all going. And if you like I can take you both on to Folkestone, rather than back here. The trains would be more convenient."

"Thank you very much. I'm quite ready."

"Good, I'll fetch my car. Ah—Miss Cole."

Stephanie was standing at the door of a room opening off the corridor.

"Yes, do go in," said the Superintendent, to Brett. "The father's in there, and your sergeant." He went off without waiting to see Brett inside.

"Where have you been?" said Stephanie, pulling the door to, so that they were shut in the corridor. "I haven't seen you since all that in the car. What have you been doing? You look awfully tired."

"I am tired. Aren't you?"

"No. I feel rather odd, though. A bit as if I'd had a tooth out. Oh, wasn't it awful!"

"Forget it. That sort of thing ordinarily happens just once, if ever, to a law-abiding person. You've got it over early."

"Well, but I didn't mean just it, which was bad enough. I was so stupid. And when you think of these things happening—or things a bit like this, anyway, you imagine you'd be all cool and collected, in fact you'd probably be the one to get people out of the mess. But when it was real, all I could do was cry."

"Everyone's like that, Stephanie."

"I didn't see you crying."

"Of course, a person like Beddoes will distinguish himself in the real thing. Did you know he boarded that helicopter and brought it down, without really knowing how?"

"Did he?" Stephanie sounded unimpressed. "Oh, have you seen the things they had in the packing cases? They're unloading them in another room—that policeman, the one that went out, he's awfully sweet, he let me go and look. Oh, you must. Mr. Majendie's nearly going mad." She stopped suddenly, and laughed. "We can hear him even in there. 'My dear good fellow! Pray be careful. That figurine—Christie's last year—almost identical—so-and-so, so-and-so—Bustelli, you know.'"

"You mimic him very well, Stephanie."

"Well, I hear him every single day. Oh—that reminds me. You remember about that cameo? Well, I thought how odd it was that Mr. Emmanuel should have let you have it cheap if you weren't a friend of his or Mr. Majendie's, so I made a few inquiries—"

"God above!"

"Discreet inquiries," she said, with dignity. "And I'm terribly sorry to have misled you, but it was fifteen all the time. It really was. After all, it's very easy to mistake fifteen for fifty, especially when it's not said to you but to someone else, and you're only overhearing. What's the matter now?"

"Nothing," said Brett, "nothing, nothing."

"I was going to tell you in a letter," she said. Her face clouded. "Now I've nothing to write about."

"Would that deter you? Take me in and introduce me to your father."

"Oh, I suppose I must," she sighed. "You know your famous Sergeant Beddoes is in there too? He introduced himself."

"Don't you like him?"

Her hand was on the door. She turned round, surpassing herself in smiles. "Not so much as you," she said.

"In short, my dear fellow," said Majendie in a low voice, puffing slightly as a result of his exertions in plodding through the snow, "you believed me to be one of them. No, no—don't apologise. It was a natural surmise. Ah—now I appreciate the force of your observation, that the Princess was unaware of the irony of choosing me, in connection with the sale. Dear me! Then you also thought that I'd—what's the word?— *double-crossed* my associates, that I'd concealed my summons to Bright's Row and privately profited to their loss. But I must positively insist, my dear fellow, that I neither bought nor stole it from the Princess. I had intended to correct you in that, was on the point of doing so, you may remember, when events began to crowd upon us—confound! This snow is damned difficult going. Treacherous. I wonder if I might avail myself of your arm—ah, thank you! No, sir, the Princess gave it to me. To be precise, she offered me the choice of what I best liked from the whole collection. I confess I was staggered. I mean to say, what if I'd picked the emerald necklace? I should have had a fortune drop in to my hand without so much as lifting a finger. However, my dear boy, when you reach my age no doubt you'll feel as I do—what, after all, is money? No, it was the collector's piece, as they say, which took my eye. Oh, there were many such, but this was outstanding—'the star of the collection', as you expressed it with quite remarkable aptness. I didn't hesitate."

Majendie paused. "The others are drawing rather far ahead of us. Shall we close up? Miss Cole, blessed girl! What energy! What a pace!"

They plodded a little faster.

"Why did she offer?" said Brett. "Was it by way of being—"

"A tip," said Majendie with startling relish. "Commission, at its highest evaluation. Nearer the mark would be the trades-man's Christmas box. The servant's reward. Oh, I was under no illusions—am not, perhaps I should say—as to my status. I took it, dear boy, I took it. And when you called the other evening with news of the robbery, I regret—no I don't why should I?—I *admit* that my first reaction was one of relief, that I'd taken away my reward and had it in safe keeping."

"That's an admission," murmured Brett, "but no news. It showed on your face as plain as the nose in it."

"Dear me!" Majendie sounded perturbed.

"And what about *Common Law and the Common Man*?" pursued Brett. "I suppose that was consulted to discover what legal title you had to a plain gift."

"My dear boy, I must remark on the sharpness of your eyes—yes, and on the imagination shown in your guesswork. You're right, I was somewhat worried. I knew, you see, that the unfortunate Ivan had seen the collection. The Princess told me so—not in the pleasantest manner, I fear—but you've thought of all that for yourself. If he had got wind of my visit, perhaps even been told of what had happened, and had pressed a claim—"

"Why didn't you ask a solicitor?"

"But my dear fellow! Suppose my solicitor had told me I'd no right to it—he would have known I had it—"

"Look! They've stopped," said Brett.

"Come on, dear boy!" cried Majendie, suddenly shooting forward with such vigour that Brett was almost pulled over. "I must be in at the kill."

"This snow—" began Brett, then stopped. He had been going to comment on the facility now shown by Majendie in getting through it. But how many, and how shocking, had been the remarks of his which Majendie had magnanimously overlooked! "It reminds me of a paperweight," he concluded tamely.

"Paperweight?" Majendie appeared to prick up his ears in the midst of his headlong flight.

"You know, the sort you pick up and shake to make a snowstorm inside."

"Ah yes," said Majendie indulgently, "charming, charming. Well, my dear Miss Cole?"

They had come up with the others. Mr. Cole and the Superintendent were grovelling in the snow. Stephanie held one torch and Beddoes two.

"Found the place?" asked Brett.

Stephanie flicked her hair. "Sergeant Beddoes noticed the snow was disturbed," she said coldly.

"Well, it would have been different if there'd been another fall since you buried it," said Beddoes, with astounding humility.

"Aha!" said the Superintendent, "here's a strike. Steady on, the lights. Some more off your end, Cole, old man. That's it—up she rises! Now, sir, is this your property?"

He held out the little dressing case.

"Yes, indeed it is," said Majendie, seizing it with joyous lack of ceremony. "Will you allow me one moment? I must reassure myself—"

Holding the case in one hand, he dipped with the other into a pocket inside his coat, and brought out a small key. He poked away a clot of snow which was blocked between the handle and the lock, inserted the key, and opened the case, revealing a watered silk sponge bag. He removed this. Underneath, bedded in cotton wool, lay a grey velvet egg-shaped box, some five inches long.

"Ah!" Majendie's sigh of relief was long and deep. He laid back the sponge bag.

"Oh wait," said Brett quickly, "don't you think you'd better make sure?"

"My dear boy—here?"

"It's as safe as anywhere."

Majendie looked at him—one of his best hamster looks. He nodded briskly, and without a word dropped the sponge bag and thrust the dressing case into the arms of Beddoes. He lifted out the grey velvet box, unfastened a catch at its side, and opened it so that the hinged halves lay flat.

Cradled in the satin lining was an egg, white, icy, its surface starred and patterned like a window pane in a hard frost, with a diamond monogram glittering in the middle. Diamonds, close set in a band of gleaming metal, encircled the egg lengthways.

"Oh, Mr. Majendie!" breathed Stephanie.

"Yes, my dear—notice the exceptionally interesting

effect achieved in the engraving and enamelling. Platinum mounts—and brilliant diamonds throughout, you'll have observed, which is unusual. But I'll open it."

The egg, like the box, split lengthwise into halves on a hinge which was invisible from the outside. The shell on the left was hollow; its whiteness was studded with tiny stars, thin platinum points tapering from single diamonds. On a white velvet cushion in the right half lay a brooch, one large dazzling star, Arcturus of the first water, darting needle flashes as it quivered in Majendie's hands under the torchlight.

No one spoke. Majendie, with another little nod, closed the egg, and the box, put back the sponge bag which Beddoes had retrieved, and closed the case.

"So that," said Brett quietly, "is the Christmas Egg."